COPPER TONGUE

PATRICK RODDAM

Published by Cut Flowers Press Ltd, 2021

info@cutflowerspress.com

A CIP catalogue record for this title is available
from the British Library.

ISBN 978-1-7399579-0-2

Cover Illustration by Geoffrey H Turner
Cover Design by Matthew Hayward
Printed and bound in Great Britain by Aquatint Ltd

Here lies caution,
shot in the back by impulse.

I

Never at night. Never alone.

The *Tooth* had no time for outsiders. Hell, just as rough for those who lived there. Suppose to feel at home in a place like that you must evolve along with the environment, kind of thing you can't fake or teach. Can't just call yourself a shark and dive into the deep sea.

I was out of my depth. Luckily it was raining pretty hard, washing some of the heat from the streets. Still I moved swift with my head down, glancing up only to show I wasn't blind — I'm not looking at you but I see you. Most fearsome creatures will go on about their business if you mind your own and stay out of their way. It's the predators at the edges of perception to be truly wary of, the ones that see you first and see *you* as their business.

The district took its name from its form, a jagged fang taking a bite back at the restless waves clawing away at it. Of course, human nature was the more immediate threat to the coast's survival. Long before a shotgun wedding shackled up a couple of singular geographical and political landscapes, other insidious seeds of greed had been planted and neglected, toxic roots breaking through in time to cause utmost damage.

Hard to believe it was so different only a few miles away. The world at large had moved on while this world had fallen backwards, and far. Temporary solutions become permanent. Decay had taken hold. No one on the outside was minded to do anything about it and those on the inside were just trying to get by. Or revelling in it.

Descent was evident wherever you looked. Everything was outdated, patched up; antiquated infra-structures kept on life support by necessity. Exposed veins of tangled cables were stretched out and nailed down. Fumes that had been outlawed anywhere civilised choked from back-up generators, rundown vehicles and the masses blazing what they had to hand. Even the light had its own distinct and shady character, viscous and provocative. Must admit I would dig the aesthetic if I wasn't the latest mark on the canvas.

Warpaint was starting to trickle down my face. Never been much of a tough guy, but grew up around enough to know how to hold up a bluff. Real deal can see straight through it though: the slightest tremble in composure; a weakness somewhere in the core; the spirit lacking in conviction.

I'm not something but I'm not nothing. That's the way I saw it and assumed how it looked from the outside too. Not blissfully unaware of the wild eyes amongst the trees but not fierce enough to stare back either. I stood out for all the wrong reasons on both sides of the divide. Fact I had already been around that same block twice made me stand out double.

Wireless didn't tend to work so good around the port; interference from maritime navigation systems, best guess. Chance upon a signal and it might stretch to a bar or two here or there, enough to make a call but not to check a map or anything like that. Wouldn't help find what I was searching for anyway.

I smuggled out my guide book, nothing more than anonymous scrawlings on the inside of a j-card from a cassette, and discreetly studied the diagram I had already memorised and already knew didn't make sense. No number, just an 'X' in the middle of the road I hoped I was actually on. Then, surveying the map from the territory, I realised why I couldn't see the spot. It was right in front of me, hiding in plain sight.

One of the old trams slugged by, crunching a gutter congregation of the shiny little malignant capsules that littered the city. I hopped a ride to the next crossroads, landing at the mouth of a red-rusted gate that on first and second sight I had thought was somehow lost, guarding nothing on a tiny island in the stuttering traffic.

The iron sighed, offering no resistance. A disused public facility lurked in the darkness below. As I took my first step down, the stone shook beneath me. This was it.

II

Rainwater salivated from the street above over the head-to-toe jaws of a turnstile in my path. As I pushed against the mechanism to no avail, a set of jagged fingers stabbed out from the dark beyond and I felt my body throw itself back but with nowhere to actually go. A pair of yellowed eyes and a grin to match gleamed in the shadows.

The hand beckoned me to pay the toll, flashing up a palm spread wide. Had some papers loose in my pocket, small bills to the front. Soon as I pulled out five sterling a single finger wagged. Rule of thumb where local was the preferred currency was to take the number and double it. As expected, dropping a *cockle* did the trick, the tender scrunched into a ball and disappearing back inside the bars before a resounding clunk indicated a good time to try the gate again.

Swallowing me whole, I noted the grinding teeth had been rigged to only revolve the one way — exit through the gift shop, apparently. Settling into the curves of a deep sink and somehow making it look quite comfortable, the gateman was not physically imposing but rather a raggedy and detached character that I doubt anyone really messed with. He paid me no further interest, not in the least concerned whether I had anything I shouldn't on my person. Presumably I did.

A lone strip of tired light at the far end led the way, hanging from the ceiling inside a wire cage. Built with the needs of tourists in mind, the lack of doors on the cubicles suggested the abandoned restroom had seen more action from natives feeling a greater need. Further I ventured, rowdier the cause of the rumbling under my feet became. I stepped into the last stall on the left and out the other side.

○

Bowing below an artless archway smashed through the tiles and two feet of concrete, I emerged into an underground bunker just as a raucous crescendo collapsed in on itself; a DJ I couldn't place jamming the handbrake and yanking a track into reverse. I got that sensation of walking into a joint and the record scratches and all heads turn. Except no one looked back. The hard-breathing horde before me, lithe and wiry, fizzed with static energy, ready to bolt.

The needle fell into the outer groove and a saw-toothed surge of bass cut me straight down the middle.

Constructed solely from substantial sonic torque, the intro that followed could just as well have been the ignition sequence of a futuristic craft that had seen better days.

The speaker system, battle-scarred tannoys far as I could tell, rumbled under each reckless thrust, threatening to cave in. Maybe a forgotten wartime shelter, the appropriately low levels of visibility made the dimensions a challenge to fathom; glistening limbs of the several dozen revellers sketching a rough map of the boundaries and intimating at otherwise hidden routes to deeper cavities.

With the tension ratcheting up to dangerous degrees, I started to detect an implied rhythm in the rugged bursts of sound. Rest of the room could feel it coming too — something big — holding their breath as all that pent-up pressure abruptly subsided to silence. I didn't move a muscle.

A sudden storm of caustic drums shredded the heavy air. Shoved just a single step forward I was thoroughly swept up. Standing still was never an option, even as I tried to hold ground amongst the thrashing debris. Despite how turbulent it must have looked, once I'd accepted that the ground had already given way and let myself go it felt more like carelessly free-falling — time dilating, contours on screwed faces and inked skin becoming defined.

Terse venomous spits into a mic echoed from every direction. With the dance getting increasingly riled by the unseen MC's harsh language, it made no sense to hang in there any longer. Could always double back once the floor thinned out some. Another single step, deliberate this time, and I was unable to stop, darting only forward through rapidly sealing human fissures until I stumbled into the centre of a six-strong circle, shadowboxing amongst themselves.

A dozen dead eyes turned in on me. From adolescent warehouse nights I was no stranger to this practice and deflected the first adeptly pulled punch that flew my way. Soon I was struggling to keep up as faux blows rained from all sides. A bit from a kung fu flick flashed across my mind, where a young buck weathering a tempest in an old monastery has to run a gauntlet of seemingly sentient wooden dummies.

No way to be sure it wouldn't get serious any second so decided to push on, targeting the smallest of the sentries. Turned out to also be the quickest and took great exception at being picked on, driving me heel first through the parting crowds. Just when I thought I might take a hit for real, the record skidded to a halt and my assailant fell completely still in sync with the inertia, like a clockwork automaton running out of turns. He span away as the vinyl was wheeled up for the second time. One last step, backwards and unexpectedly deep, and I was clear of the entrance hall.

○

A brutal wrangling of near-sheer static filled the blackened passage that lay ahead. Wading on I strongly considered turning back, but then reasoned it was just the tough skin I had to tear through to get at the sweet fruit inside.

Perseverance paid off. Wall of noise traversed, a central hub offered a handful of pathways. I checked out each scene: a scrap breaking out between slashing strings and concussive percussion; relentless chasmic kicks submerged in monochrome drones; an oddball union of mishandled instruments and roughed-up electronics; writhing body rhythms narrated by indecipherable sleaze. Good stuff. Just not why I was there.

○

When it needs to, the body reacts far quicker than the mind.

It's a survival thing; wouldn't last long if your instincts couldn't override the controls when necessary. Point being, sometimes you know it before you comprehend it. Drifting on a steely current of air through the dark, a slight decline underfoot of what was surely the most outlying of the tunnels, I became aware that there was something other pulling me onward.

Haunted hotspots sometimes turn out to have a phenomenon in common; a conspiracy of geometries that amplify deep frequencies into a presence you can feel but not hear. Can tingle the fingertips, scratch your arms and legs, or hit you in the pit of the gut. Easy to get spooked by such an uneasy sensation. There and then, it was pressing firmly on my chest, where I tended to perceive anything of significance.

Stray notes strafed by as I neared a gauze of light, soon fused by the mercurial acoustics into a weary, searching disharmony that sounded like nothing I'd ever heard. Except maybe when I listened hard inward. I merged with the velvety glow and just watched a moment. She didn't look up.

The sombre tones that enveloped the womblike chamber were born of a violin, played freely from the hip. Each aching draw fed an amp, the old and new carefully attuned to produce an otherworldly cascade; lapping waves leaving broken reflections in their wake. A barely-there pulse was thrummed idly against the body of the instrument.

More silhouette than anything else, a frame as taut as the strings she caressed, it was the fine details I was able to make out that drew me in: the thin silver spike piercing her upper ear glinting as she tracked a runaway sound, errant and apparent only to herself; a hairpin curve forming between her brow and cheekbone as she zeroed in on her quarry; the little pout of her lips as she made a minute adjustment to her grip on the bow before again letting fly. I was struck by her focus, fearing that I lacked the capacity to be so captured.

Hadn't noticed there were other people in the room. Suddenly self-conscious, I plotted to evade the handful of curious gazes from the peripheries but thought it would cause at best more attention, at worst a disruption. Decided to remain still at the threshold — I was exactly where I was meant to be. At least that's what I tried to project. Whether it was force of true will that gave me away or I shifted so subtly that even I didn't catch it, her eyes shot without warning straight into mine. Everything went black.

Down that deep, it was not simply a change in the

light you could eventually adjust to but rather instant total darkness. A few reverberations of sound lingered just a fraction longer. Severed from amplification, the exploratory sweeps of the violin were skeletal, the heartbeat hollow. I imagined she could play traditionally, but was perhaps out of practice or just plain didn't want to. The strokes became increasingly tentative until they too disappeared.

Relying on milk from the careless motherland had left the port open to bouts of deprivation. The outages were common, a whole black market springing up in response — *power brokers*, the freelance genny-ops liked to call themselves. I had no idea when, or if, a backup would kick in. The other occupants held out less hope, filing straight past me by digital torchlight.

Not one to follow, I listened to the trudge getting distant. For a time there was nothing. And then she started to sing. Softly at first, in an old tongue, as she fumbled together her belongings. I didn't need to understand the words to get the meaning. Even as her keening voice grew into the void it sounded like it might fall apart at any moment. Felt I might fall apart too.

The lament frayed from existence but I would swear I could still hear it, never certain it had ended until the distinctive flick and flash of a Zippo lit a cigarette. A firefly flittered through space towards me, chasing the wavering flame.

Drawing near, she led with a guarded glimpse of her emerald greens. Not sure how well she could see me but I didn't smile, instinctively mirroring the energy by narrowing my pale blues so slightly. Up close her features were fiercely delicate. She was a whisper of a thing, but tough with it. Kind of lass who looks after herself, no matter how hard you might want to.

She exposed her throat as she removed the Marlboro, smoke pluming from her studded nose. The coarse shroud took me all in: the aroma; the taste; the feeling as it touched my lungs; the doubting I ever really quit. I eased my shoulder back and she slung on a rucksack as she passed, catching me in the waist with that of her instrument, swinging free inside. I returned the sentiment as she faded away.

"Hey."

III

I knew where I was but not really how I'd got there.

On one hand it was lucky. After retracing steps I had found myself back at that once seething dance floor with just my phone for company, little more than a glorified flashlight in the circumstances. Chasing echoes of the dejected exodus through a dark warren, I'd reached another junction with five paths stretching out like bony fingers. I took the middle digit and was greatly relieved when it eventually opened up into another unoccupied restroom. The turnstile only revolved outwards.

On the other hand, the sight of the decaying Ferris wheel, looming like a slain colossus as I climbed out of the ground, meant I was somehow right at the tip of the Tooth. I could hear the sea and taste the salt.

The rain had relented and already you could feel the heat regaining a stranglehold, wraiths of steam rising from the slithering streets. Was a little disconcerting to find I had them all to myself but knew it wouldn't be a ghost town much longer — fire brings forth devils. Wild mood swings in the weather were to be expected on any night of the fall, the season a volatile cocktail of the flames and storms that bordered either side, but it seemed more acute on the coast.

Home was a train ride and a world away, but go far enough back and I did have history with the town. Both pairs of folk's folks had lived there all their lives and I'd spent a fair few hazy holidays with them as a child. As a teenager, me and the boys would make Saturday night pilgrimages to the promenade, trying to score with the local girls. Had my first proper kiss down by the shore; giggling with a real sweetheart from the roller rink as the tide chased us away. Tonight had not been such a success, albeit on a different kind of hunt, and with my only lead cut brutally short it was already stumbling towards the same conclusion that it did back then — the last train home.

Moonlight peppered a worn down tram in the middle of the road. A passing glance confirmed my suspicion that it had nothing to do with the blackout, most likely left for dead some time ago judging by the rich tapestry of battling graffiti crews it wore. Continuing to a sidewalk overlooking the water, I remembered all but running to try keep up with my Grandad's stride as we'd head to his favourite spot to eat ice cream and watch the waves.

Wouldn't trust my life to the crumbling barrier

these days, but the gentle giant used to pop me up on there, legs dangling over the edge. Felt like a mile down, the inward curve of the seawall unnaturally steep; only time I'd ever had a sense of vertigo. Didn't seem so far to the surf now, a determined gust of wind brimming the pavement and speckling my boots. The whole pier was slowly drowning.

A gunshot tore me from reverie. Heart beating so fast it felt like it wasn't beating at all I scanned for the shooter, eyes blurring to try pick out an offensive shape or movement. A light crested the top of the road, accompanied by a surging growl and settling nerves. Didn't think I'd been spotted or was of interest until the motorbike backfired again, swiftly mounting the kerb. The rear wheel thrust into the air as the nose slid to a hard stop a couple feet away.

The cold mirror of a visor sized me up. Wrapped in white leather, a blue and red stripe running from shoulder to ankle, the rider sat motionless astride a muscular custom mould, also in white. Bearing resemblance to a beast with its hackles raised, the machine snarled with impatient menace.

Having seen enough, the helmet cocked to one side and the tail of the bike chased, engine howling. A twist of the wrist let off a double-tap of shots, deafening at that distance, and a rush of wind passed through me like a spirit. By time I'd looked round there was no sign other than a hanging trail of exhaust. The ringing in my ears morphed into an unnerving whirring. Something else was incoming and it didn't sound like a lone wolf — sounded like a pack.

A headlight bobbed up. Then another. And another. I stopped counting and ran to the back of the tram, forcing my fingers between the flaking rubber edges of the sliding door. It wouldn't budge, the components long forgotten how to move. Kicking the glass in would give me away. No chance running for it. Nearly tearing my arms from their sockets I violently jogged the door's memory, wrenching it open enough to slip inside.

Beams swooped eerily across the metal husk. Already on the deck, I crawled to steal a look out the front windshield. A line of six motor scooters slalomed languidly down the slope; if they were out on the hunt they had lost the scent.

I'd only heard about gangs like these, young runners who decided they'd had enough of toeing the line and severed the tether of their masters, biting hands right off if necessary. Kind of hard to blame them, kids were doing all the dirty work and realised they didn't need some brute eating up the biggest cut. After one crew had shown the way, others followed.

The front runner choked the throttle and took off, careening towards the tram on one wheel. Holding improbable balance for longer than was comfortable to watch, he dropped the landing gear twenty-odd feet away. Guess he'd played this game of chicken before but hadn't accounted for the conditions. Attempting to swerve the immovable object, his front wheel slipped and wavered uncontrollably. I grimaced at the crunching impact.

First clue the runner had been thrown wide in time was when the pack caught up, circling the tram and cackling like hyenas. Their fallen leader cursed them and then his ride. From my position, prone on a natty fabric bench, more furtive views through the windows and wounds in the chassis only made the picture worse — they were younger than I had thought.

Aside from the networks, there was another valuable asset the breakaway generation had taken from their elders — discipline. Hard to acquire but then even harder to lose, the trailblazers used the fortitude that frontier law and order had harshly instilled in them to not only survive the coup but also thrive in the aftermath. The new pups coming up, such as those doing laps around my shelter, were free to the point of being feral, a product of children raising children.

Hauling his bruised ego and vehicle up, the runner made no attempt to assess what could be salvaged and wheeled it uneasily towards the sidewalk, picking up pace with each step. The scooter hobbled hesitantly against the momentum, as if trying to deny its fate, before being launched into the barrier and taking a good length with it over the edge. Not even bothered with seeing the drop, the runner spun on his heels, dusting his hands. Then he stared hard at the tram.

Responding to the gesture of a throat being slit by an index finger, the runt of the litter removed a shiny canister from a small holster-style satchel, handing it over like a baton as the runner entered the circle. Breath collected on the window I lay under while I held mine. I couldn't get any lower. A metallic click and clack preceded the toxic hiss of a red line crossing out an apparent rival's nom de plume tagged on the glass.

The discarded spray can clattered to the ground. I peeked out through the back to see the pack peeling off one by one, the leader following on foot. With a casual confidence that made clear it had been done before and often, he leapfrogged onto the pillion of the passing runt and they sped away.

Thinking about it, they should never have been there. Youngsters like these didn't tend to stick to established lines like their forebears, they had yet to come into an inheritance, but this was obviously occupied territory. Whatever they were playing at, least they were gone. For now.

○

Ever feel like some inanimate object is out to get you?

The instant I put a hand on the tram door to prise it open a little more, a hinge snapped and the heavy metal sheet swung like an axe, aiming to maim for my earlier use of force. I actually felt a pinch on my fingertips as I withdrew them in the nick of time. Now it was truly wedged shut, the askew top corner tucked inside its own frame.

Turns out it's not that easy to kick through a pane of safety glass, even if attempted with a fair amount of spite. I placed a few solid soles against the tall window that made up the core of the door, but the lack of room to manoeuvre in the entrance-well meant I couldn't really get a hip into it. All the other windows were either as equally solid and ill-positioned for an incisive strike, or narrow portholes designed only to let in a token trickle of air.

Knowing the driver's cabin could only be locked

I tried it anyway. Reaching around blindly through the little ticket hole was more fruitful; didn't find a handle but by virtue of my face being pressed against it I realised that this window was perspex. Searching the carriage for something to hit it with, something hit me — a droplet on the ear. Straddling a couple of headrests, I fought against a build-up of murky water and threw back the hatch in the roof.

First thing I saw as I pulled myself out through the compact opening was power slowly restoring in the distance. Finding my feet followed by my bearings, I watched a disjointed wave of light sweeping on across the west; a beacon for where I needed to be.

"Never gonna get anywhere standing on ceremony."

The words sounded like those in my head but they weren't. For a start, the voice was female.

"I mean, I've heard of riding the tram but you taking it to the next level."

An apprehensive three-sixty confirmed there was not a soul on the road. Hadn't even thought to look up before a movement drew me there — a pair of well-worn Chucks dangled a couple feet high and a few more wide of what had been my eye line, kicking the air. Perched on the flat oval head of a retro streetlamp that must have looked so futuristic when they lined up decades ago, was a stocky twenty-something with a shaven head.

"What are you doing up there?" was my initial concern.

"What are *you* doing up *there?*"

"Fair point," I conceded.

The enigma unravelled a length of cable from around her waist, closing one eye while peering at the loose end with the other. Her ancestors had certainly travelled far from the East, but where they had started from and stopped along the way it was hard to say. Other than the question of heritage, her face gave very little.

"Working. Big project," she mumbled, swivelling the tip of a finger-sized Maglite removed from behind her ear and sticking it in her mouth.

I hesitated to disturb her as she diligently separated the wires inside her cable and entwined them with their counterparts in another much longer length, zip-tied around her work station and stretching back to the previous lamp — and on and on from the looks of it.

"You there the whole time?" I finally interrupted.

"Mm-hm." She removed the torch from her teeth. "For a moment, when you were looking out to sea, I thought you might jump."

"What? Why?"

"Dunno," she shrugged, "got that kind of vibe about ya."

"Fuck you, man!"

She took no offence, as intended. "Just calling it."

"Wait... would you have stopped me?"

"Who am I, your guardian angel?"

Fair point.

"What about that guy in white?" I accidentally wondered aloud.

"What about her? Kitted out like that, it was definitely a *Whiptail*, and they don't do dudes."

I'd happened to catch the *Tails* before they were really a thing on an *'and finally'* news segment years ago. A diverse trio in the capital had started a women-only biker club. Cute at first, grew pretty fast. Once they counted over three hundred nationally, with progressively fringe interests, the man declared them an organised outfit.

"Local chapter's only sweet on racing though," she continued, ripping a strip of black gaffer from a roll worn as a bangle. "Whole city's a circuit, can't miss 'em on a Friday night."

"That's tonight."

"There you go," she said more to her handiwork than me, clinically bandaging it with tape.

"Didn't look like much of a race."

"Wasn't," she concurred. "By the seems of it, that Tail was just wagging the pups. Always snapping at ankles them yoots."

"Love to get their hands on a ride like that, huh?"

"Yeah, right." Job done, she returned the shining torch to behind her ear and checked me out. "Where you try'n get to anyway?"

"Home, I suppose."

"Let's guess, back in the real world?"

"That obvious?"

"That obvious," she verified. "What you doing round here?"

I considered my response. "Looking for something."

"No joy?"

"Not yet."

"Seen. So what..."

Our discourse cut dead. She became aware of it just before I did — a whining chorus of low-powered engines, some ways off but coming back. Shaking her head, the young woman stood to her full height, about five and a half squat. Gathering up her excess cable, she hurled the coil through the open window of an adjacent building. Next she pivoted and pigeon-stepped until the toes of her trainers were curling around the edge of the lamp's head. And then she leapt.

Landing on the roof of the tram with a thud that staggered my balance, she bowed theatrically, as at the end of a gymnastic flourish. I couldn't help but smile. Sporting baggy shorts and a tight tank, she was built like a boxer and moved like one too. A small but solid fist was offered up.

"Tommi."

IV

Tommi was a journalist. Freelance.

From her office window, I watched the young runners gunning for trouble back along the coast road. The tiny bureau was on the second floor of an art deco building that called itself the *'People's Hall'*. I disputed the suitability of the name but was reliably informed there were sometimes other tenants around somewhere. Wouldn't necessarily see them in the labyrinthine old establishment, but would hear them doing whatever it is they do.

"Crank this," I was instructed, a wind-up lamp finding my hands.

Grinding light into the room, taking over from the tiny torch tucked behind Tommi's ear which had seen us so far, I discovered the space wasn't actually all that small. The boundary I kept to en route to the sea view was in fact a patchwork of defunct electricals; a drystone-like formation of partially-stripped servers, screens, consoles, printers, radio apparatus, and assorted tubs of wires and ends.

The opposite *'wall'* was formed of haphazardly

stacked newspapers and magazines, textbooks and novels, stretching for the high ceiling. I wouldn't have been able to add to the pile unaided, let alone my diminutive host.

"Throw that over here, will ya?" she told me, grabbing the circle of cable that had landed square on her desk and pulling it tight against the lead window frame.

I shone the lamp from on high as she secured the slack around an ornate brass coat peg, which I'm sure had been hammered up on the wall for no other purpose. Taking cue without being asked, I lowered the glow in close as she brought the loose end to its terminus — a monstrous-looking PC constructed of snatched parts from the gadget graveyard.

While Tommi stitched the inner cores to a modem which made up the top floor of her homemade tower, I took the chance to peruse the desk, an expanse of dark wood that was either built inside the room or the room was built around it, and I would assume abandoned by the previous occupant. Other than an appropriately fat-backed monitor, more than half as deep as the slab it sat on, the rest of the workspace was covered by a rough hand-drawn map of the city.

Starting in pencil on a few assorted sheets of paper at the centre, the survey continued outwards in pen across post-it notes and envelopes, in marker across scraps of cardboard and brown bags, and even chalk across rare glimpses of the bare surface itself. A red thread linked a couple of pins, one at the southern root of the Tooth and the other at the north point, where I currently found myself.

"What's at the end of the line?" I enquired.

"That's a question, ain't it? But assuming you're referring to the thin red one there, well that leads back to the big mama. This contraption here's her pretty little sister," she snickered, stroking a tousle of tumbling wires.

"You're hooking up some kind of local network?" I figured.

"Some kinda."

I traced a finger along the route. "What is this, about a mile?"

"About a mile."

I briefly contemplated the undertaking. "That is indeed a big project, Tommi. Guess life was better when everything was connected."

She temporarily diverted a fiddling index finger to waggle it back and forth.

"You don't miss being part of the conversation?" I asked with added air quotes for good measure.

Her head shook resolutely. "All that back then was the illusion of a voice, save our souls written in the sand. This here won't wash away. I see it like carving in rock. Don't dig what I write, can't just wait for the tide to turn, gotta come tear it down."

Measured footsteps creaked in the hall, growing louder until pausing outside the door. Laboured breathing sounded as though it were right in the room, unsettling the hairs on the back of my neck, before huffing and shuffling away. Tommi carried on unfazed by the creeping apparition.

Finishing up with her task, she narrowed her eyes at me sharply — in stark contrast to the limits of her scope as it turned out.

"Town needs a library. Bulletin board at the least."

Placing a pinky and thumb on the threaded-up pins, she slowly incy-wincied an imaginary web between a dozen or so other waypoints scattered across the locales of the map.

"I'm talking notices, opinions, knowledge. By us, about us, for us. You get me?"

"You serious?"

She shrugged. "Hardest part is finding the right gear. Modern systems are too fragile, needy. What I need are sturdy scraps, enough for thirteen servers.

That'll do for starts."

"How are you possibly gonna hook them all up."

"One at a time, of course."

"So... does it work?" I tried not to sound sceptical, the wind-up running out of steam in my hands.

"See when the juice comes back on, won't we?"

Tommi's eyes lit up — literally. With divine timing, my first crank synced with the streetlamp outside the window buzzing to life, pouring in light golden and thick like honey. She stretched around the back of the computer and located the weighty thunk of the power button. Nothing. Then a dim dot on the screen accompanied by a basic but strangely emotive tone.

"It's alive!" she exclaimed, mad scientist-style.

The machines wheezed and warbled, deliberating for what seemed to me unreasonably long in return for a grid of two tones of faded green holding a single file, listed in grey text: COMMUNITY MEMORY.

"There you are," Tommi gleamed, keeping her eyes on the prize while rooting through a tub of spare parts.

"What is it?" I had to ask.

Retrieving a mouse bound by its cable, Tommi spun it overhead to unfurl the tail from the body and plugged it in.

"Entry number one, a guide to the system. How to

build it, how to use it, how to fix it when it breaks down."

Hovering the cursor over the file, Tommi turned to me, arching her brow to highlight the significance of the moment. When she looked back she saw what I had just seen — the text had vanished. She squinted closely at the screen, as if it might be found hiding if she stared hard enough, then dropped to a seat on her heels.

"Shite."

○

Taken inch by inch, a mile is a great distance.

That was the prospect facing Tommi. Two weeks of nights, dozens of precarious climbs and an obscene amount of gaffer tape and cable ties had shared a file between a remote pair of Frankenstein computers for all of thirty seconds.

Don't get me wrong, I was impressed. Hardwiring a connection over that distance, solo with scavenged materials, was no mean feat. Just saying, I probably would have called it a day at that point. To be honest, I wouldn't have started even if I'd thought up such a sprawling scheme.

Tommi considered it a predictable setback and though clearly not thrilled, was also not deterred from her mission to hook up terminals across the city. To eventually get that far however, she'd have to iron out this initial kink and that meant working back along the first mile, inch by inch.

Making our way down through the People's Hall was a much more charming affair with the lights on. Soaking in the palpable sense of the grand building's history, Tommi explained that the other server she had built was at her apartment, a studio in a 'hood known as the *Drink*. She was a legacy tenant, the hollowed out roof that had once housed her and her parents was now hers alone.

While ago, when the land was being reimagined into the future, Tommi's home and those around it faced a sudden upturn in fortune. Leaning back onto a low tumble of green, before it all devolved into the range of moors to the south, prospectors saw potential and sought to buy up properties to sell on to the fresh wave that would surely come flooding into the fast-developing industrial coast.

Tommi and her neighbours had resisted the rise of gentrification and as a reward were resisting rising waters; that prized open space is now an ever encroaching marshland. In common with much of the territory's story, the promised gold never materialised.

I'd not seen it with my own eyes so took her word that the area's reputation was largely exaggerated. Only a few low-lying streets were off-limits and a few more would get washed out by a high tide — you learned to watch the moon if you lived around there. Still it was hardly Venice and she couldn't take a water taxi from the canal to her front door just yet. In the meantime a good old pushbike did the trick.

Speaking of, she dropped to the ground as we hit the street and slid a stashed BMX out from under the stricken tram. Most bikes found knocking around were treated like burners; grab one when you need it, ditch it when you don't. But this compact piece of chrome belonged to Tommi and she intended to keep it that way. She hopped on and set off at a pace slower than walking, neck craned to study the cable running from lamp to lamp.

"Welcome to a saddle, but I'm going my way at my pace," she murmured over her shoulder.

"Thanks, I appreciate the offer. And the asylum."

She gave me a thumbs up as I watched her edge away. In the absence of any direction of my own I froze a moment, deliberating over my literal next step. Then Tommi stopped, standing still on her pedals in a cogent show of control.

"Hey I gotta ask you something," she declared without looking round.

"Okay."

She moved off at the same steady crawl.

"Go ahead," I said, drawn into stepping after her.

"I'm thinking."

"You didn't have something in mind?" I queried and gained.

Tommi took her time.

"Right. What's the best thing that could happen to you before sunrise?"

Pulling level, the wilds of possibility stretching before me, I found myself playing it safe.

"Tonight I just wanna stay out of trouble."

"Really?" she cut back quick with a sideways glance. "Hm. I think you need to broaden your horizons."

"I'll take that under consideration," I bristled a little.

"Roll the dice, man," she punctuated with a wink.

Tommi picked up her rhythm until I was no longer by her side, apparently abandoning her task for the night.

"Any more tips you'd care to share?" I called after her.

"Yep. Steer clear of the *South Road*. There be real bandits."

V

Unless you counted swimming across to the harbour and gaining passage on a freight ship, which apparently I did consider however briefly, I had no choice other than diving back into the very pulp of the Tooth.

I hadn't bothered trying to open a virtual map before setting off, electing to walk the length of the lonely promenade and hang a right when I was in line with the deteriorating light house — remembered from stomping around in the past that this would lead to the city centre. Was probably the longest route but also the most certain and I never learnt any others as there never seemed the need; the trains used to run all the way out to the water and even back when it was a family-friendly destination I avoided going downtown after dark. Now, in a far less innocent age, I was about to do just that for the second time in as many hours.

Before I got to the waypoint, a spontaneous shortcut down a half-dozen steps that I didn't see until I was passing them — a large part of their strange appeal no doubt — led to fifteen minutes of indifferent back alleys. Often found it hard to resist the lure of the oblique path, but I'm sure that Tommi's comments ringing in my ears played a role in the decision to take that particular one.

The scattering of rolled-up awnings and rolled-down shutters revealed I was in an informal shopping patch, a mix of small homes and micro businesses and both at once. Should have paid more attention to the handmade placards but the multiple languages in use meant I took in more of the colours and compositions than the content. Had noticed the graffiti on the walls repeating but that's what tags tend to do. Finally realised I'd doubled back on myself at least once when I again hit a dead end with a crudely daubed but prescient message: YOU ARE HERE.

I started to worry about time. Had no certainty when the last train would go, and doubted it necessarily did either, but guessed it would be around midnight. Took out my phone and saw it was ten-to and, to my surprise, I had a couple bars of signal. Was a mixed blessing. The map that slowly loaded clearly defined the bordering main roads but put me at the centre of a blank mass. I could barely see the sky for the narrow walls but according to the cloud I was in limbo.

It had been foolhardy to think I could just stumble about in the dark and fall upwards. Usually, a grasp of general direction and a bit of back and forth will get you there eventually. But knowing where I wanted to go didn't mean a thing to such crooked nooks; could feel my needle going haywire as I was repeatedly turned around. Unable to rely on compasses internal or otherwise, I focused on the surroundings and started to realise that the tiny streets I had thought were dead were actually just snoozing.

Subtle signs of life appeared from the dwellings above: soft shards of light teased from behind blinds by the wind rustling up a steep passage; a little courtyard scored by the crackle of an unattended gramophone running in small circles somewhere; the muddled scent of a veritable herb garden overgrowing a corner from a series of window boxes; wonder how long that black cat was skulking behind me before brushing up against my leg. Not sure who jumped highest.

After laying down a few mental markers, and a little more trial and error, a hop and skip up another small flight dropped me right on the main drag — rush hour in full swing.

○

Everyone's addicted to something — whatever you consume that is in truth consuming you — and everything of the illicit variety could be found hanging out together on the block; a gauntlet of fiends either peddling their wares or looking to score. I'm not judging. Nobody wants to go home alone and vices make good bedfellows. Cosy up with one though and there's a fair chance you'll be introduced to their associates, sooner or later.

I passed the rusted gateway that had witnessed my earlier descent, my grin of recognition met with a familiar sigh as it turned away in a breeze that I certainly didn't feel. A vintage hatchback pulled alongside. Bracing for anything as the window rolled down, the sight of the kind-faced elderly lady listening to talk radio made me smirk at my own jitters. She poked her head out the window and absentmindedly spat by my feet before zooming off.

The bulk of the human traffic flow was local. Grafters from the industrial zones spilled from pubs, glass in hand, grabbing a stronger nightcap. Party girls and boys picked up little pick-me-ups as they shimmied from one venue to the next; one altered state to the next. Moped couriers swooped in to deliver orders made via designated payphones less than ten minutes earlier. It wasn't all business though. The friction of such high spirits glancing by — laughing, flirting, squabbling — generated a buzz all its own, a tangible vibe that made the strip feel like one long open-air nightclub. Have to admit it was tough to resist strutting on that dance floor.

A benefit of the port's discrete status, if you saw it that way, was the license given for some creative interpretation of the law within its limits. Back home, wags you got chatting to at shop counters swore they were gonna move across so they could smoke again. For some the incentives kept coming: no restrictions on alcohol; b-classes were a-okay; gambling was unregulated; prostitution casual. The motherland blushed.

Regardless of autonomy, there were still some substances that were outlawed just like everywhere else. In principle. In practice, heavy gear you're only supposed to operate with the appropriate qualifications, in this case a note from a serious doctor, was no harder to get your uncertified mitts on. The country at large was developing a rather problematic co-dependent relationship with synthetic opioids, but the Tooth had a full-blown ill-fated lovers thing going on.

It wasn't so much the drug itself that had initiated the whole affair as it was a new method of delivery. Sabre rattling inside hastily barricaded borders had necessitated the invention of new means of preserving all sorts of goods, none more so than pharmaceuticals. To double its shelf life, a potent painkiller was suspended as a concentrated fluid inside small silvery capsules which inevitably made their way onto the black market. *Pearls*, they call them.

Some intrepid psychonauts ventured that once popped open, the rich liquid inside could be syringed, chased, vaped, frozen into hard candy or just knocked back like a shot for a vivid drift in a weightless wonderland — Atlantis in the palm of your hand. The catch; once hooked, the line reeled in real hard but from below. Whether you saw it as free-diving or getting dragged under you were still heading for the same deadly depths. Discarded pearls speckled the ground the way cigarette butts used to, down-and-outs dredging them up for the dregs.

All this played out in the open, no attempt made to avoid hand-to-hand transactions or conceal what was partook. There was no need. The old CCTV cameras were like gargoyles, relics from a different age that were only effective if you believed they were actually watching. The police had long since packed up their ponchos, replaced by *Blacklock*, a security contractor that had colonised the warehouse zone before their jurisdiction, to much public outcry, was expanded beyond all precedent. Can't say I'd ever seen one of their enforcement officers in the flesh.

○

Bodies like walls, limbs like bars, my need to pass seemed to make the crowds all the more determined to detain. Of course they were mostly oblivious, no way to know or reason to care I had somewhere to be, but it's animal instinct to resist any restriction of movement — one step you can't take could be one closer to getting swallowed. More I struggled against it, more the human quicksand sucked me down. I eased up.

A lot of manmade circulatory systems have an intrinsic push and pull to them. Move decisively enough and you'll quite likely get your way. Hesitate, and prepare to get stepped on. Got to lean into it, whichever you choose. Trusting my judgement, and failing that my reflexes, I moved on steadily, giving way here, pushing through there, until settling into the slipstream of some swaggering wrecking ball. Suppose over the years I'd become quite adept at dodging meaningful contact. Intentionally anyway. Every now and then, albeit in less hazardous surroundings, I'd be cruising along on autopilot and would catch myself testing the boundaries; looking too long, moving too close, pushing my luck. So far, so what.

Had been such a while since I'd really been challenged I think my subconscious was seriously starting to doubt that all the threat was anything more than just that. No sense what I'd do if I did happen to get unavoidably fronted up. Guess that thought is what made me so wary of confrontation — what would *I* do?

That night wouldn't be the time to find out it seemed, the railway bridge that marked the station coming into focus up ahead, the last train resting on the corroded horizon. Still a final obstacle stood in my way. Or rather three.

Two on the left, one on the right, all smiles. They weren't quite a matching set — a couple of tight collars opposite a loose tracksuit — positioned just close enough to a parked car and a caged shop window that you had to pass through the middle of their posturing.

Something about the space between them felt off. I slowed slightly to get a better read. First I thought they were just projecting their physicality, taking up as much ground as their egos deemed necessary. Next I suspected they could be trying to catch something in their net; waiting for the right fish to drift by. Nearing,

I spied the smaller of the two dandies shifting a heel, grip tightening around the strap of the red duffel hung over one shoulder. The lone hood bobbed on the spot, restraining some rash action, and if I could see it, they could too. Their glaring beams were really bared teeth; deal gone south, I'd bet. That space they were maintaining was really a distance between each other.

I was overtaken on the right then soon after brushed past on the left. Walking apart but together, the second stayed six feet back and six across from the first. Their urban uniforms, a close match for each other and their allegedly isolated accomplice, gave them away as a unit as much as the sync they kept. I watched them slink innocuously towards the chokepoint. It was about to kick off.

The hood fronting the sting couldn't hold his nerve any longer and made a play, catching the dandies off guard and actually taking possession of the bag for a second before being caught himself. A tug of war by the straps threatened to spill the prized contents while frenetic punches and kicks blitzed the outnumbered point man. The odds didn't take long to more than even out, a hefty trashcan launched through the air and clattering the dandies as the back-up joined the fray. I stepped into the road as the gawkers gathered.

It was a common scuffle, the sort I'd seen often in my youth and for the most part managed to skirt around. Impromptu and chaotic, there was no raising of dukes or choosing a style, just furious shouts of fierce young men dragging each other by their mangled clothes, crunching off hard surrounds and slamming onto the ungiving ground. With clean blows at a premium, elbows, knees, nails, head butts, anything was used to gain an advantage. Fortunately none of them appeared to be tooled or prepared to use it if they were. Not yet.

I zigged through the rubber-necking traffic, touched the opposite kerb, then zagged back towards the station entrance, giving the ruck the widest berth practicable and picking up the pace as it spilled in my direction. Near clear on the first of forty-odd steps up to the platform, a spindly figure in a bulky coat, slumped on the handrail with hollow eyes that didn't look to be watching the show like everyone else, suddenly peeled off the wall and lurched into my path. An inelegant vertical waltz avoided not only the collision but also the customary ire that followed — could feel his glare trying to engage but mine was fixed on my footwork so as to remain upright. Had we collided it would have been his fault but my problem.

Two steps at a time, a sincere collective gasp

from the audience turned my head to see a weathered machete whipped from within my dance partner's pelt. The street fighters halted abruptly as they could but refused to give up on the bag even as the heavily-interested third party stalked towards them. I didn't look back again.

VI

In the belly of a steel snake I crossed a concrete jungle.

The pacer trains that served the city were older than I was, a short-term fix from way-back-when that had managed to slither away from a supposedly final cull several years ago. Little more than converted bus carriages, they were slow, noisy, uncomfortable, and somehow colder or hotter than the outside — whichever you wanted respite from. I stood up through my petrified breath, lower back already objecting to the tough suspension and tougher seating, deciding to surf the uneven rolling motion from tail to tongue. Wouldn't get me there any faster but would get me away from the threatening hiss somewhere beneath my feet that pierced the frigid hull at every slight twist to the track. Besides, might as well stretch my legs; had the whole thing to myself.

I'd resisted the temptation to look down at the rapidly escalating situation on the road below as my ride juddered away, moments after I'd jumped into the last car. Much as some morbid part of me wanted to know the outcome, I already knew it wouldn't be a good sight to commit to memory, even though it was improbable the fearsome blade would need to be used for anything more than shock and awe.

Leaving the ruckus in the rearview, I walked alongside a frail arm of water and despite the mist could make out a smudged outline of the docks across the inlet. Much clearer to the eye was the dense warehouse and container complex that served the passing ships. Oblivious to the blackouts and lit up like a brutalist shopping centre, it was plain to see the priority it held to the otherwise incognito authorities. Not without good reason. The utility of the port — practically and as a theoretical lens through which the picture of international tariffs became blurred — was the whole argument for it becoming free in the first place.

Though the storage village began soon as the docks ended I couldn't tell how far it now stretched. Most likely it was still growing. So many promises of what a measure of autonomy would bring to the district and this is what they got. That and a lack of accountability as it all fell out of step. Convenient as it would be to say there were some sinister figures pulling the strings, I put it down to commonplace corruption and inherent negligence — no one was driving the car. I tugged a rattling door and finding the one on the other side of the coupling wide open, stepped across.

While I paced the middle of the three carriages, the train bisected a dark heart. The considerable wasteland that made up the core of the terrain was essentially still just that despite years of faltering factory construction — first thing you have to assemble is the assembly lines themselves. Pitched as the first brick in a grand regeneration, the never-ending building works had become its own enterprise; a *Winchester House* on an industrial scale. The native workforce toiled for the benefit of remote firms on open contracts maintaining inscrutable and often incompatible agendas, other than that of being in no rush to get the job done.

To be fair, one facility had recently become operational; a refinery for the raw ore extracted from the mines to the north. It meant the base material, copper in this case, could be exported even if it hadn't been fashioned into something useful yet — the world wouldn't be kept waiting for its motors and guns. Also meant waste products amassing in landfills and a handful of stacks coughing heavy smoke into the atmosphere.

Stepping into the front car, I drew alongside another bleak copse. The *HighWire* business park was an earlier whirl at monetising the barren area. Five towers, laid out like dots on a dice, were joined by jolly communal areas designed by committee: quaint cobbled paths; water features; enough foliage to give an impression of nature. A factory for the twenty-first century, they reckoned.

At the time, the new face in the workplace only needed a phone and a booth, and at its peak over eighty percent of the tower's units were occupied. Technological imperative never sits still, however. In a fraction of the time it took for the old generation of labour to be marginalised by their mechanical counterparts, the new batch suffered a similar fate at the hands of AI. As occupancy in the high rises plummeted it became cheaper for the landlords to let it fall dark. What was actually needed was capacity to store the mountains of stuff that consumers had to have, and towers are not very well suited to storing anything. Except people.

The compound was repurposed as *'temporary'* housing for displaced and never-placed citizens. Adequate office space does not make for an adequate home though, unless you're cosy with jagged little boxes, shared basic facilities, and luck of the draw far as neighbours go. It wasn't the country's largest or most populated estate, but it was the most crowded per head by square foot and certainly among the least liveable. Without the excessive but necessary maintenance it no longer receives, the

Racks, as it's known to those in tenancy, is falling apart; the blocks crumbling, the weeds overrunning. Wildlife is thriving there, apparently.

From my passing vantage it looked placid enough, the way a graveyard does from a distance — a bit too still and I wouldn't choose to walk through either at night. Even knowing I'd have to come back this way at some point, I was glad to be leaving the whole sorry scene in the dust. Then the train started to stop.

○

Never been much of a tough guy. Said that before.

Not that I ran away from trouble, just that I didn't run towards it either. Usually. Exceptions to the rule often occur after long periods of deliberation or in the heat of the moment. This was the latter.

From the back of the front link, the train gingerly swaying around a needlessly sharp and presumably fragile section of track, I'd watched in disbelief as a desperado jogged alongside the pacer. Red bandana concealing from his glazed eyes down, he forced the vehicle to stop at the point of a white plastic pistol that looked like a prop in an old low-budget sci-fi.

Clambering on board and ordering the greying

driver out from the booth in a booming baritone, the great train robber wanted nothing more than wallet, phone and anything else to be found in the old boy's tattered uniform pockets.

Heel to toe, one foot after the other. Couldn't hear my own breathing but it was steady. Desperado failed to look back when he got on, tunnel vision in full effect. Didn't mean I wouldn't be next. Driver saw me coming but stayed cool. Not sure what I'd do when I got there — guessed we'd all find out. Wasn't a creak under foot that gave me away but the whole carriage groaning as it leaned to one side under my carefully placed weight. Eyes looked crazed once they were staring straight at me.

Rest of the desperado's body followed his head round except for his gun arm, snagged by the driver. The 3D-printed thing went off like a party popper but it was the shooter who really made a noise, squealing as he dropped the weapon like a hot potato and hopped about the spot before falling sideways out the carriage door.

Cradling one hand with the other on the hard ground, the desperado struggled to his feet using his forehead as a brace and brayed away into the dark. Watching him go, the driver and I shared a titter that was as much nerves as genuine mirth. I cautiously probed a boot under the bench where the pistol had ended up and scraped it out to find the barrel peeled back like a banana. Shuffling it towards the driver, I caught sight of the thin arc of blood around the doorway of his cab.

"You're hit, man," I half-said, half-asked.

The driver surveyed his frame, taking a couple passes before noticing the small hole in the left arm of his thick coat and the dark red trickle making its way towards his sleeve. He quickly raised his wrist, I'm sure to stop from making a state of the floor.

"So I am," he sounded almost amused.

I looked on with a mixture of concern and curiosity as he swivelled and scoured his cabin. After a few moments hunting he snatched something off the dash and returned holding a small object in the light for us both to see — the dull metal projectile that had passed through him, to some degree.

"Imagine that," he grinned before tottering backwards and slumping into his chair.

Stepping forward with purpose, I carefully removed his sleeve and supported the arm at a right angle to his shoulder on an outmoded console.

"What's your name, sir?" I asked in a friendly but fairly firm tone of voice I hadn't heard in a while.

"Winnie. Winnifred actually, but you know..."

Glancing at the flesh wound as I rolled up his shirt

cuff, he flinched away just as quick when I pressed the edges together with my fingertips. It wasn't bleeding too bad and a bit of a run-off was probably a good thing, washing out some of the foreign material. Would need a bunch of stitches and leave a fat scar though. Could have been a hell of a lot worse.

"Folks sure you were gonna be a girl, huh?"

He nodded proudly.

"But you went with Winnie over Fred?"

"Not how it works, jack," he chuckled and grimaced a little, "you don't choose your own nickname."

"Guess not. Pinch that, would you please?"

He'd already reached a thumb and forefinger to take over applying pressure before I'd finished the sentence. I prized the antique first-aid kit off the wall and open but it was empty save for a few dot plasters. I scanned the cabin for alternatives.

"You some kind of pro?" Winnie wondered.

"No. Did a cursory course once, part of the training for the field I worked in. Got anything to drink?"

"Used to," he smiled wistfully, "flask of white rum was never far from hand. Now I'm straight black coffee."

On the counter surrounding a thermos was a dozen or so sugar sachets from various joints.

"That'll do."

Winnie looked a little perturbed. "It will?"

I plucked a navy and white-dotted pocket square from the breast of his coat; model's own as opposed to part of the official get-up and a shame to use, but it was the cleanest thing about. He watched sceptically as I poured a few shots of demerara in and around the gouge then wrapped it with the fine piece of silk.

"Okay then," he said with a raise of his brow.

"Okay then," I confirmed. "Still better get straight to a hospital."

"Hospital? Tonight?" he scoffed. "Would be busy in there as dead out here."

My expression must have been insistent.

"Look, I could either go now and sit in the waiting room for hours with the bruisers or head home, listen to some notes and go first thing in the morning. Which you think I'm gone choose?"

○

Steadying himself with his right on my shoulder, left clutching his own as if it were in a sling under his loose coat, Winnie followed me down off the pacer. I was naturally a little gutted that this was an undesignated end of the line for the last train out of town, but could hardly blame the guy for calling it a day. It was a cross-country mile to the Racks where he lived and he saw no harm leaving the vehicle where it was — someone else could sort that mess. I swished my hands in a shallow well of rainwater, collected in a vacant headlight housing on the train.

"Will clean it up real good when I get in," he promised, "A and E at dawn. What about you?"

"Where's the nearest civilisation?"

"Not where I'm going, that's for sure!" he joked. "'Bout the same distance east back where you just run from as west to the *Sleeping Quarters*."

"West it is."

"Bless, my man," he said earnestly, "appreciate the assistance. Safe journey now."

"Right on, Winnie."

We bumped fists as my hands were still wet. We'd turned away when a thought hit me.

"Hey, what if you run into that desperado out there?"

Winnie kissed his teeth. "He'd better watch out!"

After our laughter had quietened down, and many paces apart in different directions, he started to whistle a tune, some sort of jazz lullaby. I knew it from somewhere.

VII

Winnie's gentle tones had disappeared into the breeze around the time the mist rolled in, heavy enough to grab handfuls of. Walking the tracks no longer seemed such a good idea when I could only see a few feet ahead so I'd taken alongside. Shock wasn't a risk as the pacers ran on diesel, and as such there was probably even less chance of being snuck up on even if one did happen to be passing in the night. Still, my instincts insisted on caution.

Away from the hustling streets it felt unnaturally cold. Ploughing on through the darkness, I realised I was thumbing a sharp corner of the j-card in my jacket pocket. The map on the inside fold, hand-drawn in diffused slashes of black crayon, led me to conclude it was significant, along with the fact the cassette it was supposed to be wrapped around was missing like the person it belonged to. But it was the cover that intuitively drew my eye; a greyscale rendering of an indistinct figure in uncertain terrain. Didn't need to take it out to remind myself how it looked — I was living it.

I'd been spun more than once already that night,

but realising the rails had vanished I finally felt lost; must have unconsciously drifted beyond a sensible distance. With no visual cues to anchor myself in the sea of murk — couldn't even see an outstretched hand — I found some comfort in the rough ground underfoot confirming I was at least upright. Checked my phone in good faith but no bars, no bombshell. The digital compass was working though, assuming it was true to begin with, and apparently I'd listed a little north along with my west so I corrected course.

A chill began to slowly exert a grip around my neck and it had nothing to do with the weather. Vision compromised, my hearing had come to the fore, its aid not entirely welcome. Knew I wasn't alone out there but had made some peace with the sporadic scuttling of harmless little creatures trying to mask their runs under the bass of my steps, even if they did scratch at my nerves with each darting movement. It was far more unsettling when they fell still and silent.

A harrowing scream suddenly cut through everything. I froze to the spot, held by the shivering howl as it rose with the wind. It felt not of this world, rendering me completely numb as the undoubtedly immense being veered between fearful and angry and sad and all at once. Only after it died away did I regain a semblance of control over my faculties, forcing out a nervous laugh as I scrambled together an explanation.

I'd happened upon an urban legend that turned out to be true. I vaguely remembered — many years ago, around Halloween probably — skimming an unusual article about the HighWire. Workers were complaining of a strange wailing, manifesting most when the weather was tempestuous. Some of the more susceptible souls rumoured it was the ghost of a call centre operator who had thrown themselves from the very top on the very first day it opened for business.

After a handful of employees had quit, reportedly due to the recurrent phenomenon, the developers reluctantly responded to the claims, trying to appease the faceless companies renting the space rather than any sensitive individuals, I'm sure. They pointed the finger at a design feature of the central tower, which served as both a nod to the complex's moniker and to help it tiptoe up to the tallest building in the region. An asymmetric mesh of high-tensile wires crisscrossed the roof via a series of spires at erratic placing and of varying lengths. Damn ugly, by my estimation.

When gusts caught it just right, this cat's cradle-like formation of essentially giant instrument strings would sing like a demented aeolian harp. I always thought the whole thing unlikely; even if the curio did exist could it really be that distressing? I stood chastened. Can only imagine what it sounded like up close let alone from up high in one of the towers. Guess the new residents of the Racks had learned to live with it.

Though I'd reassured myself, I still hadn't moved since the scream stopped me dead. That was about to change — rapidly. Fast feet rumbled inbound; couldn't tell how many or from what direction until I could hear the grunts and see the large shadow bearing down. The spooked eyes of a porcelain white horse stared straight through me before I threw myself clear of its indiscriminate flight. I was still on my back when the galloping hooves faded away, winded and unwilling to move. Harsh hailstones that arrived in a hurry got me going.

The rocks pelted down, stinging my ears and lashing my fingers as I covered my eyes. Hopefully couldn't keep this up for long but was so intense I stumbled several times as I hot-stepped it. Don't know what I was rushing for, not as if shelter was going to appear out of thin air. Until it did.

Looming through the gloom was a huge structure, so out of place it took a moment to make sense of — an excessively wide on-ramp leading up to a sawn-off section of sky-bound highway, held aloft by a pair of sturdy stanchions. In my state of mind it struck me as like discovering a giant fossil, perhaps the hips of an ancient demon, complete with tail. I got underneath its span as quickly as I could to find the sanctuary already occupied.

○

We were about the same age but his eyes had seen a lot more.

A small campfire flickered across the serious features of a visitor from the Middle East, failing to bring much light to the furrows formed from years of troubles. He sat motionless, watching me close. While I considered what I could say to or which movement would acknowledge that I was aware I had encroached on his space, he seemed to read my intentions and lowered his gaze in a subtle but resolute gesture.

I crossed my legs opposite him and my interest was piqued by the unusual but highly pleasant scent of the golden liquid gently bubbling in a repurposed catering-sized tin. Whatever was brewing wasn't to be found anywhere near the wasteland, surely procured on one of the many arduous steps to this refuge — maybe even all the way back at the point of departure. Everything he owned in the world was gathered around him in neat piles, essentials that by necessity could be carried alone.

Beyond the syncopated percussion of hailstones rattling overhead and all around I could just about make out the intermittent shrieks from the Racks. They no longer seemed threatening, now paired with the low hum my host would respond with to each call, finding harmony as if trying to soothe a restless child.

Reaching into a worn leather satchel on his lap, he pulled out a ceramic cup adorned with an intricate pattern in a rare shade of blue. Gripping the thin brim between forefinger and thumb to counter the lack of a handle, he dipped himself a tot from the makeshift pot. After a moment's contemplation he pulled out a second cup, the same ornate motif but in rose, a hairline fracture running from the base to a missing chip. He passed my refreshment around the fire, placing it on the ground before me. I dropped my head in thanks for the second tea I'd shared that day.

○

Hadn't slept well the night before. Not sure if I'd even slept at all. I mean, I must have, can't have been lying there awake all night, but it felt that way. Was up ahead of the sun and walking the streets where I'd grown and returned to after the life I'd fashioned in the capital started to unravel. Wasn't going anywhere in particular, no real purpose, and ended up at Val's just because she was peeking out her blinds as the day was peeking over the rooftops.

Only fifty-something, Val had started young; a single mother when still full of youth herself. She was a little wise and a lot of fun, straddling the line between parent and pal somewhat. The open-plan kitchen, where I assumed she spent most of her time, was the central hub of her housing association-owned lower-ground flat. It was a warm room, decked out with pictures and knick-knacks. Hadn't been redecorated in a while. She and her boys had lived there in some combination for as long as I remembered. Maddison, the elder of the two, was in my year and we used to play out when we were little. Stayed connected when we went to different big schools. Really drifted apart when it came to higher education.

I liked to think that I looked out for their family, especially since Maddy was no longer around, but in truth, the more days that passed by the less I did. Feeling antisocial, I might have gone out of my way to avoid bumping into her if they'd actually been on my mind.

Normally Val talked and I listened. About the news, what was on TV, her friends, she could go until I was waiting for a sliver of air to politely interject that I had to be off. I didn't mind, time was one thing I had to give since I'd left my job, going on a year, but you always have to make a move sooner or later. That morning though she was strangely reticent, her usual patter disjointed, clearly distracted by the window. Eventually I asked if she was okay and it all came right out. Her youngest hadn't come home for a spell. Kofi had moved back in again due to circumstances beyond his control and been partying increasingly hard over the months since. Wasn't out of character now for him to be gone all night or even two, Val hoped he might have met a nice girl, but a whole week without even a text back was pushing it. She didn't want to call the police in case it drew attention to something he shouldn't have been doing, which given his recent illusiveness may not have been out of the question. I doubted they would really look into it though, even if she did.

Excusing myself to use the bathroom before I left, I poked my nose into Kofi's business. Easing the handle open I was met with a row of clothes hanging like curtains across his doorway. I quietly swept them aside and stooped in under a portable rail. Place was a state, but just being forced to cram adult accumulation into childhood digs was a large part of it. Would have a lot more space to breathe if he got shot of the piles of records that stretched from the base of the walls across the floor at steep angles. Could fit all that music on a chip the size of a fingernail these days, but who am I to talk — I'd unloaded at least half that stash onto him when I left for my studies.

Evidently his latest return was seen as an unfortunate stopgap; making do and refusing to unpack except for the things that really mattered to him. In lieu of a desk was a capsized wardrobe, and other than my old 1210s and two-channel, still going strong apparently, there must have been more than forty cassettes laying around its reassigned top. No sign of the bulky retro yellow walkman he used to always carry, which come to think of it, I'd fobbed off on him at some point too. Each tape was a bespoke item of varying levels of craftsmanship and en masse read like a survey of the contemporary underground. Despite the vastly disparate aesthetics they all started to blur together — except for one that kept calling out to me. The image drew my eye and the hand followed. Curiosity about the object rattling loose inside opened the case. The map and the treasure, a single pearl, found their way into my pocket.

Hopscotching across the clear patches of carpet back to the door, I stood on a corner of the duvet and dragged it half off the unmade bed. A slim novel slipped out onto the floor. I picked it up to put it back but was intrigued by the cover, the obscured face of a Japanese woman sleeping below a night cityscape. I fanned the pages to a bookmark a third of the way in, thinking I'd read a line about where he'd got to but didn't get that far — the piece of card being used as a marker was a two-week-old train ticket to the Tooth.

While I'd have to wait until after dark, I knew from before I'd even said my goodbyes to Val I'd be venturing across the soft border that night.

I played around with the pieces all day — the ticket, the map, the pearl — trying maybe too hard to make them fit. Painstakingly pinching and scrolling around a bird's-eye of the district, no up-to-date street view available, I found a junction that roughly resembled the little diagram from the j-card. Even if X didn't mark the spot, he might have been there at some point. Had to start somewhere. Kofi was only a few years younger but I'd always thought he looked up to me a bit. Guess he'd got the impression I was going places. Budding in the same patch yet under quite different circumstances, I was one of the few who had a good chance of becoming *something and he was always sweet about it rather than bitter. Often wished I'd lived up to the hype.*

I could do something now though. Force myself from my comfort zone and see if I could find Kofi out there. Ironically, it was as a result of the first and last time I'd got tangled up in a web that I felt a sense of duty to him. It was my fault that his half-brother wasn't there. Not that anyone else knew that other than me and Maddy.

○

Don't know when the white horse arrived under the displaced on-ramp. Maybe it had been there all along, skulking in the shadows until the hail had eased. Wandering past us, the stallion slowed and snorted at the Easterner, prompting a friendly pat on its side. Though not bound to each other, they were apparently acquainted.

I hadn't given up on Kofi, not by a long shot, but the night had been a bust and it was well past time since I'd first tried to call it. Gradually standing, I only became aware I was absentmindedly checking my pockets for something to offer in return for the hospitality when I noticed my host shaking his head; no eye contact but a soft smile. I owed him one.

VIII

A short trek southwest of the devil's pelvis lay its spine — a detached length of overpass half as wide and twice as long as a football pitch. Before the full moon highlighted the expanse, I'd heard and been guided by the signs of life that were soon discovered to be teeming beneath its sweep.

In the same vein of my recent acquaintance, a whole community were using the concrete vertebra as a roof over their heads, maybe a couple hundred of them if I had to estimate. A tent or two was the focal point of each plot, the ground loosely divided to accommodate the group's varying needs — more bodies and stuff you had, more space you got. Some of the larger ones even had sheet metal, appropriated from the industrial zone no doubt, secured as wind breakers for their exposed flanks.

Majority of the allotments were dormant, just the odd figure tinkering amongst an extensive collection of plastic containers, another couple stretching their legs and sharing a roll-up, a few more keeping the fires going — all assessing the stranger in their midst. I responded in kind as I walked carefully through the centre of their world; the faces in the shadows had come together from all corners.

The haphazard methodology that had left these disjointed construction artefacts hanging around was typical for the territory. Bet there were more out there. Far from the project being abandoned, it just meant they were coming at the task from several wrong angles. I'm sure the scattered pieces of elevated highway would eventually join up; was the idler option than levelling the whole distance and made too much sense to have a direct link between the storage complex and the motherland — then the whole area could really be one big bypass. At some point the humble homes I was passing would be disturbed, that was for sure, but it didn't mean they couldn't come back once the work was done. Long as no one cared they were there, which certainly seemed the case, then they might even get more real estate.

It's not as if I couldn't hear it coming, but was still surprised to find just how alive the settlement was at its core. The central third of the belt was a market place, packed with small stalls and people milling and chilling. Accompanying the chatter and chuckles in a dozen different languages were the musings of unusual instruments; percussive, wind and stringed. It was a peculiar ensemble, the members spread unevenly and each keeping their own tune. Somehow it made sense though. They weren't jamming but they weren't not jamming either.

Aromas from huge bubbling pots and sizzling whole joints mingled mid-air. Other counters had decent selections of fruits and handmade pastries, a couple more were like those little kiosks in busy cities that display junk food staples. As with the menu, everything else on offer had been acquired by foraging downtown and beyond for goods that could be sold direct or if not fashioned into something first — choose from an old baseball cap or a freshly knitted beanie. Speaking of which, it seemed that trade was a widely accepted form of payment. I saw a shaky patriarch finish stitching a woolly hat and shuffle straight over to swap it for an orange, that he then swapped for a chocolate bar with a vendor already wearing one of his creations.

Pouncing on my preoccupation with a table of what I gathered to be solar-powered chargers, a small boy up way past his bedtime nutmegged me with a punctured ball as a couple of bigger kids chased after him — the purest iteration of the sport. This drew the eye of a hawkish woman in a fine black and gold wrap sitting atop a stack of fabrics. I'd been aware of her presence, acting as master of ceremonies for the night, her colourful pronouncements riffing throughout the background music. She cracked something about me which tickled those who understood it.

I didn't mind. All the attention made me feel kind of like a movie star, especially when an old dear grabbed me for a polaroid selfie. She held my hand tight to make sure I waited until it developed — both our eyes were shuttered by the flash, her mouth wide open in a delighted grin. Suppose I seemed exotic in the circumstances; there was no one else quite like me around there. Apart from the guy walking towards me.

There's no good reason for why I initially tried to ignore the other outlander. My instinct was to shout hello but was quickly superseded by a sense I'd been caught somewhere I shouldn't be; I think a small smile of acknowledgement might have escaped before I put on a blank. Subtly taking stock of the lean figure somewhere in his twenties, wearing just a tee, cargos and slip-ons, it became apparent how familiar he was with the place. Perhaps that was it — made me feel even more like a tourist.

Stopping at the closest stand so we wouldn't have to pass, it turned out I'd picked the wrong one if the aim was to avoid interaction. While I browsed a collection of whittled pipes and antique matchboxes, the stranger slid in next to me. Stood shoulder to shoulder, I watched from the corner of my eye as he nodded at the owner, who reached under his crate for a pack of smokes. Couldn't stop my neck craning for a better look as the customer fingered through a sheaf of thick papers and handed one over. The tobacconist studied it a second before banking it — the local currency could be quite quickly discerned as genuine but took a fraction longer to confirm the value.

Slapping the pack against his palm, the smoker slowly arched his frame down and around until he met my sideways glance and I couldn't pretend we hadn't made eye contact. I turned my head to him — his bearing resembled a question mark.

"Alright?" he inquired vaguely.

"Yeah. You?"

"Cool, cool," he replied, already on his way. He didn't notice the piece of paper floating out of his knee pocket.

"Uh... excuse me," I called softly as he kept going.

I stepped after him, scooping up the loose leaf and seeing the denomination was a five before tapping him on the shoulder. I held out the de facto bank note and he stared at it blankly. Got the impression that his eyes were always somewhat dazed.

"You dropped this."

"Oh..."

He took the scrap with his right hand and reached around his back to stuff it in his left rear pocket, removing an old clipper lighter in the same motion.

"Kindly," he mumbled while firing one up. "Not seen you around here before, have I?"

I declined a cigarette. "No. I'm new in town, I guess."

"Hm," he responded and nothing more.

"And you... come here often?" I asked to break the impasse.

He shrugged. "Closer than walking to the shop."

"Closer to where?" I couldn't imagine.

He drifted for a moment then returned with a notion.

"Have you got a spare two ticks?"

IX

I impulsively trusted Bim for some reason but that didn't mean he knew where we were going. Lending a hand wasn't a condition of him showing me the way to the border 'hoods known as the Sleeping Quarters, said he'd take me straight there if I didn't have the time or inclination, and that's probably why I agreed to help the guy out with a two-man job first. After twenty minutes of following him back through the fog I was seriously starting to question my decision.

Right as we'd set off from the overpass I asked Bim about the note I'd returned to him, and possibly because I wasn't from those parts he launched into a fragmented history lesson. Frequently thrown off track by the act of stopping still a moment to recall either the story or the route before steering us in another seemingly random direction, he managed to relay the key turns in the emergence of the city's secondary currency, just not necessarily in the right order.

The linear version begins soon after the port gained its new status. An overseas start-up went through the correct channels and offered a local pound to the area, all based around their proprietary app: *Slip*. There was no hard cash involved; prospective *Slippers* were invited to add funds to a virtual wallet for use with small businesses and peer-to-peer transactions — swipe to pay as you *Slip* out of a cafe or bump fists to *Slip* some dough to a pal, that kind of thing.

Was slow to catch alight with the people on the streets but made much sense to the merchants eligible for the scheme, offering discounts and other incentives for choosing the payment form to entice customers out of the chains and back into their stores. There were no handling fees to be paid unless a balance was transferred out of the system into a fiat currency — long as the loot stayed circulating around its small world then there were only benefits. Presumably the developers earned interest on the total sum held on the platform, even when direct commissions weren't being gained. Eventually it took off in encouraging enough fashion for SLIP PLC to buy a license and a building downtown in preparation of opening their flagship bricks and mortar bank.

A year in and out of the blue the bubble burst; turned out to be another tech company operating at a loss until the investors called time. All support was withdrawn, crucially leaving no way for the money to be removed — an estimated million effectively trapped within the app. Financial watchdogs made the right noises about holding the shysters to account and they still are. Sounds like that's all they'll ever do.

This much was fairly common knowledge — unlike how the city eventually went from a failed virtual economy to its own physical tokens — but Bim's unpredictable delivery kept me engaged and passed the time. Literally two ticks after I asked how much longer until we got there I saw the shadow of our destination up ahead.

○

First thing to hit me was the heat. The blistered square structure in the middle of nowhere was large enough to house a few small aircraft, but the sight of hundreds of blinking servers in long lanes of steel racks stacked high made me think its original incarnation might have been a factory farm. Coat straight off and with a new appreciation for Bim's choice of attire, I followed him along the outside edge of the space to a narrow entrance into the grid.

There was no route through the middle, had to walk all the way to the end of a row then snake back around in the direction you just came from. Large fans were set up at each junction but only really served to push the hot air about like *red winds*. Aside from excessive warmth, the machines kicked out an aural haze. The gaggle of generators outside were a mere buzz compared to the drone of the hive. Couldn't help but notice Bim dip, swoon and rotate his neck slightly as we progressed. Thought he was limbering up initially, but further in I started to hear it too — curious lone tones and warped chords emerging from the complex mass. I replicated his movements as best I could and discovered he was conducting tiny sublime melodies out of the noise.

A loose note flittered free of Bim's back pocket, hovering in front of me a half-second before I snatched it out the air. The same one in fact. I handed it back again.

"Oh right... so... Big Ann, she lost it."

No clue what he was talking about. After giving me an empty beat to respond, he turned to walk backwards, holding up the repurposed cheque with a thumb under the signature strip which I could now gather was signed by *'Anita'* something or other.

"She lost her phone and then she really fucking lost it," he elaborated. Sort of.

"Big Ann?"

"Kind of a mayor. Holds a gallery space in the *Sleeps*.

Was already making the most racket about getting our money back. Got a big voice. Big everything. She's a... full lady... Big Ann."

I tried to warn Bim before he bumped into the sturdy wall of hardware at the end of the passage. A little startled, he bounced off and continued facing the right way.

"Like, it still worked. Knew the app might crash any day, but meantimes we could pass the cash in there. No one was keen to see it any more though of course. Then she uh..."

Bim slowed to a stop and tilted his head to one side, not moving for several moments until he spoke again.

"What was I saying?"

"Big Ann."

"She was one of the ones trying to keep people using it," he set off again. "Saying someone would have to sort it out sooner or later. Until she lost her phone. Did I mention that part?"

I nodded as he looked back.

"Found out you couldn't just sign into your account on another various. Think about that. I mean, you might misplace your purse, but it doesn't carry the added risk it's gonna breakdown and lock you out, right?"

I shook my head as he looked back.

"Could mean a loss of a few quid for some, several thousand for others," he mused, registering he was still holding the slip and tucking it inside his T-shirt pocket.

"And it's not even like a lucky sod is gonna find it on the street. It's just gone, forever. People carried their phones less for fear of dropping them. And I'm not saying for certain that 'cause we weren't using them so much the operators didn't care about us when it came to upgrading the networks and that was the start of getting left behind to where there's little point carrying one around now anyway. But it is a possibility."

Keeping up near enough and turning into the next aisle, close to the middle I think but can't be sure, my ears locked in on a shimmering high frequency that sounded like I imagine the sensation of pins and needles would. Half-way down and sat on the ground was a server, box-fresh save a few scratches around its base.

"Here we are," Bim pointed at the machine, "got this far but had to concede defeat."

Looking to the heavens as he pulled his cargos up and tightened the drawstring, the task at hand became clear. There were six vertical levels of the labouring drives and he started climbing the scaffold housing towards one at the top that lacked the telltale operational flicker.

"Must have had a lot ploughed into it," he sniggered. "She was already leading demonstrations daily outside their never-opened headquarters, trying to abracadabra shame into action. Now I'm not pointing any fingers, but the lady was there pretty much every day, so it's a fair bet she was knocking about to see a bunch of dead stock being dumped in the building."

Using the cover of finding a firm hold, I gave the frame a few tugs to check it was sturdy before starting my ascent.

"Strange it was," Bim spoke from the summit, "all those branded polos, key chains and other useless bits of tat showing up around town straight after the break-in and burn down. Anyway somehow, no fingers, Big Ann got her hands on a big box of blank cheques. Really blank, no customer names or nothing. Design prototypes or something."

I sized up the drives as I scaled past them; about the same as a suitcase stood tall, but wouldn't find out if they were empty or overpacked until gravity had a hold. Could have gauged the one on the ground if I'd thought of it far before meeting Bim at the top.

"See the handle?" he asked.

I couldn't, but located it by feeling around in the gap between its neighbour.

"Oh and she found her phone by the by, back of the couch, but had already made up her mind. Held a town hall for the community leaders and the scheme spread by word of mouth from there."

We edged the dead server to the end of the rack, then gripping it with one hand and the steel with the other, lowered it to the lip of the row below — heavy but not quite excess baggage. Propping it at each level before climbing after one at a time, we duly reached the base and a breather.

"Wasn't just for the full amount either," he unpredictably picked up again, edging the next part of the job into a starting position with his knees. "Transfer your balance into her account and she'd actually dispense a mix of fives, tens, etceteras, writing in the values and signing them herself like the chief cashier. You with me?"

"Let's do it."

Reversing the process to get the replacement to the top went surprisingly smooth until the last leg, when a little rubber foot got caught and for a desperate instant the machine teetered on the edge before one more heave had it sliding back into its berth. While Bim reached around to connect it, I headed for a seat on its predecessor.

"Tipped over a few months in," he shouted. "Enough people were using the cheques... *slips*, they were already known as by then... persuaded the rest to sign up. Didn't really have a choice. Was either that or wait indefinitely for the motherfuckers to sort out some compensation. I still didn't get round to it until quite some whiles after that."

All hooked up, Bim pressed the power switch and rested a palm on the top of the unit, waiting for a sign of life.

"And here we are with an exclusive and finite currency."

"Scarcity increasing the value," I speculated.

"Long as we all see eye to eye on it," he agreed, looking disapprovingly at the unresponsive machine.

"But that one you dropped is from a real bank, no?" I was fairly sure.

He hit the top of the server and a sequence of lights flashed across the cutouts in its casing before settling into the same arrhythmic pulse of all the others.

"Aha!" cheered Bim, turning to make his way down. "I was one of the very last, when she'd run out of the official unofficial slips and started using her own old chequebooks."

He jumped the last two levels, patting his heart as he straightened up. "Been hanging on to this one for years."

"Worth more than usual," I reckoned.

He smiled and winked then became comparatively serious for a final thought on the matter.

"But you know, there's one thing that no one ever talks about. Big Ann is still sitting on that fat wallet. True it can't be used now, but if a way to cash it in came about..."

○

Lugging the expired drive all the way back through the network was already burning my arms before we hit the cool air and I discovered that Bim's definition of just a little further meant bringing the thing right around to the rear of the structure. He explained there were usually two others that ran the site with him but they hadn't showed. I asked what they were doing there but he didn't know, or at least that's what he said; just paid to keep the things ticking over. I tentatively enquired if anyone knowing about the mining operation was a problem and he read between the lines, answering with a question — *would I even be able to find the place again?*

Reaching a corrugated annex as big as a small cottage, Bim, who to his credit had done the majority of the backwards walking to this point, manoeuvred us side-on to a pair of metal sheets on hinges. Without instruction as to what would happen at the end of it, he gave a three-count and kicked them open. I followed his lead and swung the server, letting go because he let go, and it landed inside with a damning crack of plastic. The space was so full of discarded hardware that the latest addition wouldn't allow the doors to close until stuffed in with a firm heel.

I declined another cigarette and as Bim lit one up I saw that same slip poking half-out his breast pocket, flickering in the breeze. I nabbed it before it made another break for freedom. He stared in mild disbelief as I offered the five back to him for the third time. He waved it away — guessed he was no longer meant to have it. I folded the unique piece of the city neatly in half and slid it in with my sterlings.

As I caught my breath and Bim smoked, shaking the acid out of our limbs, the disturbed contents of the shed creaked like my joints. Trying to ignore it at first, Bim soon confessed he hadn't the foggiest what to do with all the burn-outs. He asked why I laughed. I told him there was someone I thought he should meet.

X

The Sleeping Quarters were wide awake. While the nebulous area was considered fairly tame relative to the live wire Tooth, the nickname was more a nod to the four main communities that staked their flags and lay their heads within its spread. Not that there was any formal division, the groups crisscrossed more than the mesh of streets and the dense central square was a cultural riot, but you could tell from the vibe of establishments and concentration of dialects when you were in the North African, Eastern European, Southern Asian or largely Irish neighbourhoods at the westernmost fringe.

The Sleeps, as my guide referred to it, was the comparatively welcoming face of the city. Buffered from the turbulent downtown by the industrial wasteland, linked only by the erratic train line and a single road to the south, it was close enough to the edge to thrill but not so close you might fall. Dewy-eyed outsiders liked to picture themselves in front of the flourishing urban art or just mill about the boutiques dotting the lower levels throughout the mass of residential rows. By day it had become a bit of a checklist item for the savvy traveller. By night, the territory reverted to the natives.

"Drink?" was the first word Bim or I had uttered in a while, since his ring road route saw us rediscover civilisation from the north in the form of a threadbare football pitch that was really only identifiable by the knackered goalposts.

Despite our chatter fading after he'd animatedly recounted scoring a late winner in a local tournament summer just gone, celebration and all, it hadn't been awkward. His cuts had made short work of a low-lying suburban estate and in addition to his qualities as a navigator, as we moved down through the sprawl proper I found myself glad of his company. Reminded me of Kofi.

"Probably shouldn't," I answered nevertheless, wafting through the thick yellow smoke pouring from the door of a solemn tea room.

The majority of households were dark and quiet but you would still think it was midday rather than after midnight judging by the amount of people out and about. In contrast to the nocturnal animals I'd witnessed earlier, these cats were cooly going about their business — browsing, exercising, just hanging out on balconies and steps. It was a surreal sight; made me wonder about those sunless winters in Arctic countries. Maybe this was just the time the denizens had the place to themselves and their internal clocks had fallen in line. Thanks to twenty-four-hour licensing across the whole enclave, businesses could keep whatever hours they pleased, and of course that meant there was no shortage of watering holes.

"Sure?" Bim followed up, crossing behind me.

"It's kinda late," would have sounded more convincing if I didn't have to speak up to be heard above the overflow from a bubbling juke joint that had pedestrianised a chunk of the block.

"Come *ooon*," he pressed, the words carrying through a large stone arch into a cobbled mews.

The echo of our steps highlighted my lack of response. About half-way down the strip of converted stables I could make out something curious up ahead — a visibly heavy moisture hanging in the air on the other side of the mirroring archway.

"I don't know..." I mulled as we merged with the patient but insistent mizzle, my resolution not wavering but still going through the social motions.

Bim had smiled, winked and waved at a good few people, but once we moved definitively from north to west — from funk to punk — he was clearly in his element, near enough greeting everyone we encountered and effectively communicating with homespun sign language. Combined with the rapid barometric shift, it felt like we'd passed through a portal into a different world.

"Last chance," was an accurate description of the *Nine Bar*, literally the final stop in town before it abruptly tailed into the wretched stretch of highway back to reality. The bus service didn't bother after hours but I could knock out the ten miles home on foot.

It was hard to distinguish between the dampened music sounding all around and I hadn't sussed we were walking alongside Bim's local until he'd made his friendly ultimatum and pointed up at the creaking sign — the name in red above a pyramid of three black dice, the formation atypically repeated by the white dots on their faces.

To feign willing I glided a hand across a window pane, wiping away the misty film as if basing my decision on whatever I saw inside. My hand pulled away sharply, a shiver shooting through my whole body like I'd seen a ghost — sitting in profile on the other side of the glass was the girl with the violin. She didn't look round.

Bim eased up and barely touched the door before a wave of heady ambience seemed to throw it open and washed over me. Can't say I struggled against the current sweeping me away.

XI

All heads did turn this time. Well, nearly all, a few committed drinkers couldn't escape from their glass chasms to acknowledge Bim along with the rest of the regulars. For a different reason, same went for the one person I actually wanted to make eye contact with; sat alone at the middle booth, head weighed down by a heavy thought. I kept her in my periphery as we crossed the dance floor, dead save for a young couple, locked together and swaying gently to a funereal march led by a live unholy trinity of drums, double bass and sax.

Landing next to Bim at the bar I realised I hadn't really taken the place in, too distracted by the shine in the corner of my eye. In the motion of hopping onto a stool I took a casual inventory of the room but was again let down by my vision trying to focus only where it really wanted to, leaving most else a bit of a blur. Was enough to get a sense of the space.

Adjacent the door and running the length of the windows, the other four booths were occupied by a fresh-faced crowd, piled in five or six deep, wooden slabs in front of them just as stuffed with empties and butterflied crisp packets. Oblivious to or just tolerant of their exuberance, the more experienced patrons congregated on one side of the floor at little round tables of two or three and the odd loner. The opposite flank was a low and spacious stage for the band.

The dive turned out to be much bigger than I'd assumed from the lowkey exterior, even before I looked past the bar itself to see the second room beyond; not quite a mirror image but still a decent size. There was a more serious vibe to the clientele over there, largely severe looking characters in small groups — business discussions with associates I'd wager. At the centre and drawing a fair share of attention was a card game. One of the participants was a man mountain, his knees resting against the edge of the playing surface though he was sitting naturally. He looked suddenly in my direction, catching me in the act, and let out a whistle so piercing it cut everything for a moment except the music. He held up two fingers to the grizzled bartender then dropped them to point at me and Bim.

"Friend of yours?" I really wasn't sure.

"Big brother," confirmed Bim, the distinction hardly required.

Soon as the cork came out of a tan stoneware jug retrieved from under the bar I instinctively recoiled from the potency of the contents. I felt intoxicated just by the fumes when the duo of shots were poured out in front of us. A couple dots joined up in my mind; the back room and bootleg double proof made me reasonably certain I was sitting in one of the old speakeasies established during the *lost spring*.

"Cheers Cam!" Bim raised his spirit as well as his voice, though I doubt anyone other than me actually heard it.

Was only courteous to also salute the apparently benign titan but he didn't respond, maintaining a slightly unsettling passive smile while waiting for us to knock them back before nodding and returning to his game.

At first it wasn't that bad. The stiff brown liquid was even coarser than the scent suggested but didn't seem to burn my chest like expected. We clinked a wordless post-drink toast but I barely felt the bump. With alarming speed the edges of the world softened and I cottoned that my soul was probably on fire but I was too numb to feel it. Bim put his glass down on the counter followed by his forehead.

I needed at least a minute too but did my best to remain composed. Inside I was spinning like a gyroscope but knew from experience that didn't necessarily mean it was showing on the outside. Used to think I was an open book, that what was happening on the pages was so black and white that anyone could read it. Maybe a questionable belief that I could see right through others had led to an assumption that it worked both ways. Over time I decided it's more subjective. While most people are preoccupied looking for a mirror — reflection of the self consumes beyond all else — some really are intuitive or good with non-verbal cues. But there are no mind-readers. Take being tipsy for example. Long as you're not slurring, stumbling around with your eyes going in different directions, then it might well not be so obvious to everyone else. Mind you, holding perfectly still in the middle of a bar is hardly inconspicuous either.

○

Couldn't have been floating all that long but nonetheless touched down with a bit of a thud. Stretched out my back and arms as if that would clear the fog. It didn't, but did reveal I had grown considerably in the last thirty seconds or so. Had to remind myself from time to time that the skinny kid in which an outsized amount of weariness had cultivated was milk-cartoned a ways back. I was still a bit of a lean cut but big enough. Truth be told, due to my bearing, physical and otherwise and undeniably shaped by the questionable company I'd kept through my youth, I was more capable than most to get by in such a town. Main thing separating me from those on the other side was intent.

Leaving subtlety on the bar I braved a good look. My age give or take, she was perched at the edge of the booth, rucksack sitting opposite her to dissuade unwanted company. Surprisingly sensible black shoes pointed slightly inwards, flimsy cream socks barely covering her ankles. A partial outline of her slender legs could be traced up a vintage maroon dress to a grey hoodie speckled with multi-coloured dots, covering half her short auburn waves. Her elfin features were perfectly framed and it may have been a trick of the low light but her skin glowed a soft rose gold. For all her nonchalant style and mysterious allure she was far more than the sum of her parts — the vitality radiating from her was invigorating.

Arms folded on the table, I think she was tapping an irregular rhythm with her nails; what she would add to the backing track. A crumpled Marlboro packet lay amongst the remains of much of its contents in a bulky ashtray, silver Zippo stood to attention next to it.

Bim resurfaced with an already lit cigarette

between his lips somehow. He withdrew his reflex offer to me of a smoke almost before he'd made it this time and was nonplussed when I actually reached out for one. His expression became even more quizzical when I declined the use of his clipper. I looked over my shoulder for one last recce and he followed my line of sight. I could tell from his tone of voice that he was shaking his head.

"Your funeral, guy."

Without another second to think myself out of it I was up and on my way. Balance once again all my own responsibility I felt shaky — couldn't tell if it was the spirit or my resolve. Told myself to feel my boots on the ground. The distance across the dance floor couldn't have been more than twenty feet but it felt like twenty years. Fact the middle of the room was so empty made my approach obvious to everyone who cared to look.

Half-way there a hip youngster popped out from his group to try his luck with the same basic opening ruse that I was going for. She waved so dismissively in the direction of her lighter that he didn't even follow through, skulking away with his unlit roll-up. That's when I knew I'd been here before — stunned by the new colour I'd discovered until finally gathering that all and sundry could see it too. Never in quite the same way of course, but they saw it. Surplus pride had often blocked my path. Not this time.

The music stuttered to a stop and my steps became the loudest thing in the room. Too late to turn back anyway. I stood in front of her in deafening silence a moment before she made circumspect eye contact and I clocked the flicker of recognition and a touch of intrigue too, even if she wasn't quite convinced of my bravado. The dashing of freckles across her cheekbones caused me to falter. She held out a slight hand covered in faded little scribbles but the only thing the open palm really said was *'what?'* For a second I thought it was my heart pounding before I absorbed that the double bass had started thumping out a dangerously high pulse. I tucked the cig behind my ear and just as the drums kicked in took her hand and whipped her up.

"Hey!"

I'd never jived before in my life but didn't dare stop. Knew everybody was staring but only cared what she thought. Judging by the look on her face she wasn't sure. Wasn't sure what I was doing either, my hips apparently possessed. I swung her arm as I led backwards across the floor, holding her hand loose enough that she could pull away at any time. She didn't. At the centre I gave her a twirl and she reappeared with a wicked grin.

I reached for her other hand, finding it already on the way to me, and she bent low, kicking her heels. I joined in and wasn't the only one — most of the kids and a fair few grown-ups hit the deck as the saxophone sprayed flames haphazardly across the room. I couldn't believe how fast the whole place caught ablaze.

Girl could really move. Had no idea how long I'd be able to keep up but would die trying. We bounced off other pairs, the scene a cross between a ballroom and a mosh pit. Both of us got bumped from behind and our grips slipped along each other's forearms. Drum solo rumbling, she wrapped her fingers around my elbows, fixing me in a close hold and a deadly stare. I matched her energy much as possible but blinked first, footwork I could no longer see tangling briefly but notably before I recovered. She laughed, abandoning her serious persona, and rested her head against my chest. I put my arm around her waist and pulled all of her in tight, keeping her on those toes by dipping this way and that as we toured the floor.

The band was in full swing when the first punch was thrown. First punch I saw anyway. Was all such a blur and I'd thought the two heavies rocking with their mitts on the other's shoulders were just really into it until one leant back and let fly. For a surreal instance there seemed to be an equal share of people dancing and fighting. Haven't the slightest how it started, but once I saw Cam launch some thug clean over the bar from the other side of the dive the balance had officially tipped. Just as quick as the aeronaut staggered up Bim put him back down, crashing the pitcher of liquor over his head, and then was promptly set upon himself by a three-man crew. While the band choked out an involuntary death rattle before finally letting go, I returned the girl to the booth before heading back into the scrum.

Without breaking stride I weaved through, straight to the trio lashing down at my crouching companion. Without thinking I pogoed into the air and shoved a foot into the middle figure's lower back, bowling them all over. Bim jumped up largely unscathed and tried to pull me with him on his way out but I could see the attackers had found their feet and were coming in hot. Confrontation was unavoidable. I was surprised as they were that I didn't move.

The one I'd booted down took centre stage, bounding towards me mouthing off. Was very tall but very bony, legs looking like twigs in his skinny jeans. As he got close I slammed a shin into his knees and they buckled sideways, bring him down to my level for an elbow right into his hollow jowl. From his barrelled physique it was obvious the second one lifted a hell of a lot, even before he clasped me by the shoulders. I threw a straight jab from the centre of my abdomen, the only thing I could really do and it turned out the only thing I needed, catching him perfectly straight on the chin. His eyes fell back followed by his considerable bulk. Third guy hesitated. I feinted with my right and his left went up. Feinted with my left and up went his right. I kicked him plum in the nuts and that was that. I was fucking untouchable. Until I took some knuckles to the nose.

Caught me off guard. Covered in moonshine and fragments of ceramic, the thug tackled me hard to the ground. I was too stunned to mount a response, any sense of focus out the window. Luckily his first shot missed entirely, though I felt the wind and the crack as he smashed his hand into the floor. In obvious pain he still hammered blows with the bottom chunk of his fist, catching me smart on the ear, then the temple. Next blow was bound to hit a critical and I must have closed my eyes because I didn't see the girl thrash her ruck-sack against the side of his head but certainly heard the crunch of wood and snapping of strings from within.

He fell off me and she grabbed a hand, helping to hurl myself from the ground. She led to the exit, pushing past the innocents scrambling to get out. Last thing I saw as I looked back on the way through the door was that young couple — still locked together, still gently swaying.

XII

Sorrow was her name.

Forgive me, know that sounds unashamedly gothic but it's true in a manner of speaking. Caoin, pronounced akin to *queen* in the old Irish I'm told, but here corrupted through the course of her years to *'Kay-oh-in'* as she laid it out phonetically, variously meant kind and refined; fair and delicate; a satisfyingly smooth surface; things of that nature. In her case though it was derived from *Caoineadh* — meaning elegy. She already seemed a little surprised at herself for having given up the full form, something she didn't tend to do I assumed, and in any case it was too soon to delve into who gave it to her and why. Whichever, I thought it was beautiful. It suited her. Told her as much.

"Fuck," she blurted out, reaching into her rucksack after somewhat brusquely letting go of my hand.

We'd stopped running and started talking after putting some breathing space between us and the brawl — not so much about distance but rather twists and turns through back alleys. First thing I asked was what to call her and maybe it was nervous verve but she revealed all that etymology without coming up for air. I didn't have to respond with a story of my own name because she didn't ask what it was at that time.

Stepping into an alleyway with a wooden deck, ducking under an arc of water from an overflow pipe that trickled through the thick uneven gaps in the planks to patter on the ground quite some ways below, she found a low seat on top a discarded bedside cabinet to properly assess the damage. The violin came out in one piece. Technically. A procession of shards and wedges just about held together by the strings, broken bow and all, slowly emerged kind of like a tangled puppet. She dangled it in front of her bittersweet gaze before reaching between her legs to open a drawer on her makeshift chair and laying the carcass to rest inside. She sat there a moment, leaning against a cartoon skull and crossbones painted on the brick behind her. Feeling responsible I tried to find words of condolence.

"Had that since primary," she spoke first.

"I'm sorry," I replied with a drop of the head.

She snatched herself up.

"Why, weren't you listening? It was from school, thing was a piece of shit," she uttered, chased by a pang of guilt on her face as if it shouldn't have been said within earshot of the object. "Still a faithful servant I guess."

After kicking the coffin shut she continued along the passage, expecting me to follow and I did.

"So... I don't want to make things worse, but for what it's worth that was quite a sound you drew out of there, wherever it originally came from."

"Ta," she replied a little coyly, a slight pause as she looked back allowing me to catch level.

The creaking underfoot gave way to the stubborn stone of a repurposed loading bay. The warehouses on raised levels either side each advertised themselves to differing degrees as galleries, ranging from a neon window display to a large menacingly carved 'ENTER'.

"Where did you learn to play like that?" I asked.

"Didn't really, just intuition. Trial and error. Thing had been sitting in a closet for yonks since I last mangled *Frère Jacques*. Fuck knows what happened to the little box she used to live in."

"What made you pick it up again?"

"Felt the need of an instrument. Was using only my voice before, looping it in the same way, and got to the point where I had to move on. Evolve or die, you know?"

She steadily grew taller than me, pacing at about my shoulder height once she'd reached the top of the ramp.

"Sure."

103

"Was the closest thing I had to hand and it worked... if I say so myself."

"I'd say so too," I affirmed, scaling the low wall as she turned through an open shutter that took up most of a frontage.

We walked straight across the middle of a huge industrial gallery. The decor was severely dilapidated, purposefully so more than likely, and empty aside from a scattered twosome of brutal sculptures, all salvaged metal and vaguely humanoid. Couldn't tell if they were works in progress or the finished article and would believe either.

"You know, not to speak ill of the recently deceased," she said discreetly, a gentle brogue to her tones that I hadn't yet had the pleasure of, "but I reckon in the case of the violin it was more about the method than the tool. Time to try something new."

"Probably got a couple parts of my old recorder somewhere, you could have that," I joked, hoping she'd take it the right way an instant after the words left my lips.

"Don't beat yourself up," she smirked, "old girl could hardly have wished for a more rock and roll send off. Where'd you learn to tussle like that anyway?"

"Oh... I didn't really."

"No?" she sounded sceptical, which I must confess made my ego do a cartwheel.

○

Less a door and more a hatch at the back of the gallery opened to the central square of the Sleeping Quarters. It felt like stepping out into an arena, the commercial and residential blocks surrounding the public space standing tall in place of bleachers.

There was a lot to watch from the windows and multi-tiers of balconies, walkways and rooftops. Several bars and late-night eateries spilled onto the stage, tricky to tell how many and exactly where they were, what with the al fresco areas blurring into one another.

Older folks, engaged in classic pastimes, sat on cushions along the low walls beneath a snaking covered pathway. A younger crowd in plain white tees stood in a disciplined formation, undertaking a self-defence class. Most dazzling was a game something of a cross between football and badminton with even cloudier objectives than such a combination would suggest, forced to scatter as a parade of Whiptails drove straight through with no concern over invading the unspecified pitch. Due to the bustle to get out the way I didn't see the Lone Wolf but certainly heard the distinctive shots from her overpowered engine — as did everyone in the radius.

Caoin gently tugged my arm to stop at a mobile vendor she seemed familiar with and bought a couple bottles of beer. The beaming round fellow threw in an appetiser each, a kind of bite-sized deep-fried bao. I ate it in one and couldn't tell quite what the mix of savoury and sweet was but could have eaten all he had in the cart. After clinking lime-stuffed bottlenecks and taking a swig, the dripping cold beer went straight against the throbbing side of my head. I was amazed to discover the cigarette was somehow still tucked behind my ear, albeit with the filter hanging by a thread.

As we strolled, the absence of any formal music was not immediately apparent, compensated for by the clacks of dominoes, the synchronised training exertions, cheers and jeers from the match, and predominantly an almost harmonic ambience generated by the nightlife. Deeper in I started to perceive some strange and faint strands amongst the heavy textures. Not sure if Caoin was following the sound or was subconsciously drawn to it but we ended up in front of a busker sitting pretty much in the centre.

The fiddle, homemade on the road, had an oblong olive oil can for a body, the wispy strings stretched up a thin long neck perhaps fashioned from the bare weeping tree the player was crouched upon the roots of. He was advanced in age and extremely small but solid; had a strongly grounded quality about him. Not to mention a lustrously coiffed moustache. Stubby fingers nimbly conjured melancholic riches from the humble vessel. You couldn't just take the same elements and produce the same effects; both the instrument and the playing of were imbued with a magic refined by time. We downed our drinks while waiting patiently for the piece to finish, not that I think the wordless ballad really had an end — a music born of and as a companion to endless uncertainty — but he sensed it was time to address his audience.

Caoin pointed at the fiddle then rubbed her forefingers and thumb together. The busker shook his head then lowered it when she produced a handful of slips from her bag. She didn't dwell long before walking on but I stopped her with a soft squeeze of her wrist.

Despite focusing on adjusting the pegs, it seemed to me the busker's real attention was firmly on a better offer. I took out all the sterling I had, loose and in my wallet too, separating a ten in case I needed it and offered him the rest. Was more than enough to keep him going for some while. He met me with a wily glint and raised a hand. A single finger wagged, then pointed below my belt. I patted my jean pocket and felt the outline of my phone. His eyes, an unusual tint of violet, keened. I took out the device and held it up. He nodded. Caoin shook her head. I looked at the screen and it unlocked, ready to serve.

Probably appeared like I was idly tapping a few keys, as if pretending to evaluate the deal that there was no way I could agree to, but in fact I was navigating straight to the factory reset. My thumb hovered over the kill switch for less than a second before I hit it. With the slab of premium metal and glass rebooting, minus our shared memory, I handed it over. Don't think any of us could quite believe it.

The busker pinched the corners of a piece of ivory-hued linen from the ground in front of him that had yet to receive any donations, using it to swaddle his craftwork before presenting it over. Caoin cradled it like a baby. I waggled his hand but he was more interested in what was in the other, already prodding away at his new toy. We had walked off when he hollered out. Turning back, he waved us to stand closer together. The camera flashed.

Stopping in a passage with a constellation of glimmering stars of folded foil dangling from the pipes and fire escapes above, Caoin peeped under the cloth and tickled the strings, a warm smile on her face.

"Gotta say, that was the dumbest thing I ever saw anyone do. Love it."

"Ah it was nothing," I honestly felt. "What price a moment?"

She raised her eyebrows and nodded in consideration, wrapping the instrument up and tucking it into her bag.

"See here, there's a place I need to be but... have you got something to write on?"

I checked my pockets and found a loose piece of paper, passing her the recently acquired one-of-a-kind *Big Ann*.

"Where did... you are full of surprises, you."

She removed an eye pencil from her pocket and held the slip against my chest to write a number on the back in expressive black strokes.

"When you get a new phone, call me sometime. There's one line and like, forty people in the building and even if you get through I might not be there so try again, cool?"

"Cool."

She folded the slip and tucked it into the pocket where my phone had been then walked away briskly. I watched her go. Then.

"Um..."

She turned to my mumbled call, walking backwards to see what I said next.

"What are you doing *now?*"

XIII

Never went out of my way to ignore sound advice, but didn't learn I was on the South Road until we got out of the vehicle.

Where we were was a reasonable question in the circumstances. In trying to appear ready for anything I'd taken *'a gig'* as all I needed to know when we set off. Caoin hitched us a ride back east and I'd kept any uncertainty to myself as we rode upfront of a pick-up truck next to a genial stoner with a bushy white beard and bottle-thick glasses.

My mind was so preoccupied guessing in vain what lay ahead I tuned out much of their conversation centred on the psyched-out dub vibrating from the radio. Of course, my mental wandering may have been nudged further than usual by the first hit I'd taken in several years, a long toke from a neat blunt no less. Would have been rude, and perhaps more damningly a prude, not to. At some junction along the secluded twisting lanes, all small talk had stopped until Caoin unexpectedly designated a place to pull over.

I graciously accepted a parting gift of a generous

bud for later as we alighted at a desolate and seemingly arbitrary spot. With our ride chugging towards the coast one way, the dark road we'd come from stretching back the other, the spectre of the industrial zone above us and endless fields below, I thought it a fair time for a follow-up enquiry.

No sooner had the answer come and my clouded mind registered something alarming about it, four whooping horseman, modern outlaws with stetsons and hunting rifles, burst from the shadows two on either side riding hard after the heavy-revving wagon. Even if the raiders did run down the pick-up it was nothing more than an opportunistic highway robbery; at worst the poor geezer would have to walk home a little lighter. That's what I told myself. Nothing I could do to help anyway and we didn't stick around to see what happened next.

Strangely, that wasn't even the point we started running. We'd slipped into the high crops and trampled far enough that you wouldn't know there was a road anywhere nearby when I first thought I saw someone. Just a glimpse, a suggestion of a shape — couldn't see far through the softly whistling thickets. Dismissing the sounds of hurried movement as my imagination over-firing worked less the louder, closer and more frequent they got. I was already so thoroughly unnerved by a breathless panting I almost jumped out my skin when a hooded figure howled past us.

Primal screams bellowed out all around. More bodies came too close for comfort and we took off at top speed. As the wheat thinned I started to see them more clearly. One here. Two over there. When Caoin let out a caterwaul of her own, eyes closed, neck craned to the heavens, I realised it wasn't them but actually *us*. Ten of us. Twenty. Forty. Going so fast it felt more dangerous to slow down than speed up, my own shout was involuntary, the gasp of air and awe when I saw and heard the gathering in the clearing ahead expelled with force as we tore down the steep slope towards it. Caoin laughed elatedly. We flew through the night, an eclipse of moths drawn to a flame of a different nature.

○

Fire raged, the noise so searing it was hard to breathe. Two abused synthesisers bled out from a wall of speakers apiece, either side a stage of cobbled rock. Not sure how such a thing could be rigged up, let alone the electronics, but could sure as fuck feel the consequences—a relentless pummelling of the senses; the musical equivalent of S&M.

Couldn't see the preacher woman through the couple hundred undulating disciples, flocked to that razed swathe of earth in search of sermon. Delivered in harsh yells and hushed moans, the voice was in turns frightening and seductive and always from the very fibre of her being. The words — probably political, certainly aggressive, possibly dangerous — were obscured but in no way irrelevant, rather pitched purposefully low to lure you in close where they could strike with the deadliest effects: convert or kill.

Occurred to me that the convulsing shards of tortured signals fighting for their lives midair was not unlike a hellish version of Caoin's sound. No wonder she was so into it. Locked in an alternate groove to the one I teetered on the edge of, she leant back and I gladly took all her weight, what little there was of it, falling in with her.

O

We claimed the best seats in the house. Several groups had retreated from the furnace to the outskirts of the clearing but our spot was special — a perfectly round six feet across of wild oats latticed flat like a tiny basic crop circle, secluded enough but not so removed that you couldn't make out the metalheads that had taken over the stage. Actually sounded quite soothing from that distance, the barbarity filtered out into ethereal strains.

On top of that Caoin fiddled with her new instrument, trying to play the busker's theme from memory, the uncanny motif a challenge to recall let alone recite. She took each fumble in good humour, grumbling then shaking it off before starting again.

In the absence of rolling papers I discarded the broken stub and emptied away all but a pinch of the cigarette, mixing what I kept with the sticky gifted bulb that was practically glowing in the dark. It had been a long time since I'd actually strapped one and my hands were shaking from just funnelling and stuffing the mixture back into the hollow paper cylinder, so the lack of a *slim blue* probably saved me some blushes.

"What do you do?" she wanted to know out of nowhere.

I'd noticed Caoin had a curious little tic of sorts. If you drifted, even a beat, she would lean forward sharply, just an inch maybe two, pushing you to stay focused and pulling away the chance to plan a socially acceptable next sentence. Had to listen intimately and respond spontaneously.

"Nothing. Ditched the path I was on. I'm in the process of figuring it out."

"Aren't we all?" she followed with an adorable understated simper.

"And yourself, can you live on music alone?"

"I don't really do anything else, but that's hardly a straight answer."

Right then she got it, her fingers finding the rhythm in that way only possible when you stop thinking and let physical instinct take over. Her mouth opened wide, surprised at herself. I nodded along, genuinely impressed.

Makeshift joint ready to go, she methodically raised her frame, keeping the sinuous loop going, and walked on her knees the short distance to me. She thrust out a hip, dropping a glance at an askew patchwork pocket that I only then saw was cut from the hem of her dress and sewn back on just below her jutting bone. I carefully reached in and removed her Zippo, brushing the lid open against my thigh one way and firing up the flint as it passed back the other — an old trick I know, but reckon I managed to pull it off casually.

I took the first puff then offered it to her. Dipping forward slightly she almost lost her balance, and her rhythm, and decided that wasn't going to work. She shifted on the spot a few seconds before turning her back and leaning it against me. I placed the joint between her lips, removing it when her eyes eased open. Again she gave me all her weight. A contented sigh escaped from somewhere inside me.

"What was that?" she asked quietly.

"Ah it's just..."

Her eyes darted up.

"Just found the answer to a question I was asked earlier."

"Namely?"

"You."

"No, I mean what was the you know what don't tell me," she swerved mid-sentence, "trying to cut down on sugar."

We giggled. She nestled her head between my collarbone and the corner of my jaw and I returned the joint to her lips. As she exhaled I reached across her to take another drag, leaving my arm gently crooked around her neck and resting on her shoulder. Her playing naturally petered out and we sat in silence, staring at the stars. I felt her breathing, slow and deep.

Moments by their very definition, indifferent to how perfect or otherwise they may be, all come to pass.

○

"Hey, Kay."

The voice was a dead giveaway, but there's a good chance I might have known who the gatecrasher was without the verbal cue. Didn't actually see her before, or the approach for that matter, yet stood firmly within spitting distance I recognised the same fierce energy that I'd recently witnessed scorching the field.

"Vee, hey!" Caoin roused.

"Fuck's this?" the vixen, thirty thereabouts, queried with a trace of a Scandi twang.

"This the fuck is..." Caoin shuffled to look up at me, "what *is* your name?"

"Jack," was my answer straight back. First thing that came to mind. Can't say for sure why I didn't give the real thing, but do know I was unsettled by the cold blue stare and the chill in the wind that coincided with its arrival.

"Vanda," introduced herself in suitably spartan manner.

Serpentine braids were bound across her skull, so naturally blonde it was practically ashen as her flawless skin. Much of her figure was hidden beneath an oversized throwback tracksuit, the bottoms tucked into boxing boots laced most the way up her calves, but she had striking poise, physical and otherwise.

"We live together," Caoin revealed, waving at an entourage of six or so that had stopped forty feet short of joining us, the clique returning a lively chorus of *"Kay-Kay"s* and *"Kay-Oh"s.*

They were all young and beautiful. If ever I resembled something like them once upon then I certainly didn't know it at the time. Felt old to concede in the dark from that range it wasn't immediately obvious to me which were the boys and which the girls, their drinking circle a mass of twisting bodies and slim limbs wrapped in denim and leather, topped off with ambiguous cuts.

Vanda measured the paces into our sphere and lowered slowly to her haunches. A tight white singlet under her draping top showed off the tattoo on her neck, a series of sharp black scratches from all angles, at once chaotic and purposeful. What I could make out of her physique was formidable, most notably a visibly strong core — looked like she'd been sculptured from marble. Blessed genetics played a role, was clearly from warrior stock, but she must have worked at it too and that unsettled me some. Despite her apparel, I doubted she trained so hard for the sake of sport.

Was about to offer her the joint, but the action of her reaching for it prompted me and removed my arm from Caoin's shoulder in the process. Would have been quite provocative to put it back. Vanda took a long pull, about half of the half that was left, and plumed an arc just over our heads.

"What you think, girl?" she asked, finally diverting her gaze.

"Killer, babe," Caoin smiled, eliciting one back.

"Where did you find this thing?" Vanda referred to the fiddle, plucking it out of Caoin's cradle in exchange for the smouldering remains of my handiwork.

"He got it for me, from the *Square*. We've had quite the night."

"Oh..." Vanda studied the instrument, "is that where you met?"

"At the *Nine*," Caoin replied. "Actually... we kinda bumped into each other earlier, at my show."

"You were in the *Ashes*?" Vanda returned to me.

"Mm-hm," I confirmed, just learning the place's name.

"I play there. Also made some... how would I say... *muzak*, for the corridors, perhaps you came across it?"

I nodded. Made sense.

"That's where we met too," Caoin mistily recalled,

"few years ago. Blew her amp in the next room and we ended up playing an off-cuff set together. Closer than ever since."

Vanda held out the fiddle, just far enough away that Caoin had to propel herself off me to retrieve it.

"Vee put this whole thing on," Caoin imparted, leaping right in to a lilting piece of improvisation.

The appropriate words of acknowledgement for the host that I hadn't quite formulated never got the chance to exist.

"You shouldn't be here," Vanda left out there alone long enough for me to take personal before adding, "none of us should."

She glanced over her shoulder as a playful scuffle broke out between two of her cohorts then straight back to me.

"We are off-limits. The powers have struck blood and so claimed this vein. Sheared the surface, ready for surgery."

I might have flinched if I wasn't so subdued by substances as Vanda reached between my feet and pulled up a flattened stalk from the ground, yanking it towards a small dark object removed from her pocket and releasing a jarring scrape and thunk as the switchblade slid out of its body. The head of the crop was unceremoniously severed.

"You're trying to save Mother Earth?" was the conclusion I jumped to.

Vanda knifed a seed into her mouth, chewing on it while she dissected the rest.

"Hardly. She is already dead. Least in our lifetime."

"Then what do you want?" I asked with a little snap, deciding it better to puff up my chest than try hide. Caoin lingered uneasily a moment before continuing to strum. Vanda considered her position.

"Take this city. You are not from this place but you have seen it, how the foundations have been allowed to rot. Some look this way with sympathy, pity, shame, but I see opportunity. You cannot replace the decrepit systems one brick at a time, they are too big. But if the whole thing should collapse..."

With a handful of seeds, Vanda discarded the husk and closed the blade but it stayed in her hand. She appeared to enjoy the sound and proceeded to open and close the mechanism. Thought it was random at first but then discerned she was providing a rasping percussion for Caoin's strings, instantly giving the innocent tones a sinister edge.

"You think it's time for a reset? Start counting again from now?" I put forward.

Her head shook emphatically.

"Forget counting. Everyone wants to close the drawbridge once they are inside the castle. It's understandable. But you are never really safe, always someone plotting outside. Those structures, the social contracts we are forced to live by, they are tenuous when you look at them close. Power is a confidence scam. It's all up for grabs, so take as much as you can hold. That's how we made our home. Right?"

"Right," Caoin concurred, focused on her fingers.

I wanted to check in with her somehow, gauge where she stood on all this, but even still sat within a few inches she felt increasingly far away. I had though detected more slight hesitations in her playing during the discourse, she was definitely present, and I took it as a sign that she might not be so committed to her comrade's manifesto. Then again, could have just been what I wanted to believe.

"Doesn't that mean it can be taken from you too?" I contended.

"Of course. Look," Vanda paused, forcing me to do as instructed, "see something you think you can take from me then come, get it."

She didn't react in the slightest as two of her crew smashed beer bottles together in a shower of suds and glass, fencing theatrically with the jagged hilts much to the amusement of their peers.

"Truth is," she continued, "most people are kept from getting what they want... no, *need*... not by external barriers but by the wall within. That's what really holds them in place. Conquer it and do as you please. Just bear in mind, once you do it's even harder to get back behind it."

Vanda sheathed and pocketed the blade. I realised she had been crouching perfectly balanced the whole time, not a single quiver.

"So this here's actually some kind of occupation?" I took from her logic.

"Not quite," she mused. "Majority of these fine young citizens are just out for a good time. Maybe wouldn't be if they knew quite how much the old man didn't want anyone playing on this lawn. But here they are and that's a start. Maybe they'll make something of themselves yet. For me though, this land grab is too close to home and I won't be next. Tonight is a statement of intent. A message."

"Which is?"

"Simple. Fuck you," she growled from her diaphragm, deploying a fraction of the force used in her performance. It rattled my bones.

Caoin had stopped playing I'm not sure when and

was peering into the skies.

"What is that?"

Vanda and I heard then saw it too, a small drone buzzing high overhead, hovering a moment before swooping away.

"Time to leave," Vanda met my eye again seriously, "you both."

XIV

Deep in woods that fast surrounded, I felt less lost than I had in some time.

Was a little surprised at being all but ordered to see Caoin home, even more so that her route didn't take us back to the road but instead cross country. Though I was informed for future reference there were a few viable trails, a coastal dirt track being the most conventionally accessible, the one we took was direct from our point of departure. Also happened to be her favourite.

I'd soon got the sense that the local landscape was a dense mottle of unchecked ecosystems pushing up against each other. Further east, the ground had squirmed underfoot and the increasing presence of reeds made me wary of wandering into wetlands, so the slight diversion south into a deceptively sparse tree line was welcome. Once inside, it made me think of those vertical drops of the ocean bed, where shallows suddenly plummet two miles straight.

Despite the moonlight struggling to penetrate the gnarled knots we wound our way through, her movements were calm and fluid and I found myself floating freely. The heavy dose of hydroponics I'd ingested may well have had something to do with it, but the surreal journey was incredibly serene, magical even to be taken in by the forest's embrace. Suppose it helped being safe in the knowledge I could confidently follow Caoin's lead. Not from anything she said, rather her intimate interactions with the environment. The gentle palms and tender fingertips weren't just for support or feeling her way in the settling dark. Looked almost ritual, confirming our passage. She knew these trees, reading them like natural signposts.

Much as Caoin told me about her residence along the way I was still arrested by the sight. A relic of the seventies, the concrete construct appeared unexpectedly — one step no other man existed, next I was stood in the heavy shadow of his endeavour. Essentially a robust two-storey cube, large blocks of fluctuating size and placement, some housing frosted glass bricks, cut in and projected out on all sides including the roof, linked by pillars and beams. Even the base was irregularly raised from the ground.

It was a free-runner's dream. In my early teens, the go-to pastime when checking mates on estates was the visceral thrill of traversing the urban playground, long before we ever heard the word *parkour*. Designers of the time have to shoulder some blame for accidentally enabling all manner of risky activities; even the forecourts of self-professed staid public buildings from the era often possess elements reminiscent of a rudimentary skate park.

Around and I'm sure also under the moss and climbing vines was decades of graffiti. Nothing such as accomplished murals, only crude proof of pilgrimages made, often for no more reason than because it was there most likely, daubed across every accessible inch which due to its unique topography made for a vast multifaceted canvas. As is common in human history, the jaded paint would be long outlived by the scores of carved efforts — symbols and slogans, declarations of love and hate — none more prominent and permanent than the given name in foot-high letters adorning the uppermost frame: LA MOLECOLA.

The concept behind *The Molecule* was easy to grasp; a virus infecting a fertile host, intent on spreading until nothing remained to overwhelm. Irrespective of the pretensions of the inception and morality of its fruition, the effect was undeniably engaging, the kind of starkly ornate and forceful piece that tends to either compel or repulse. Whichever way you looked at it the thing had been built to last. Despite the more susceptible extremities withering from natural exposure and lack of intervention, the bulk had held together admirably well.

The long-term survival of the project was however intrinsically linked to the very fight it had started. The brute occupation of the land had once bullied nature aside. Supremely patient, she watched as the disease became isolated; the grey failing to spread, the green slowly but surely reclaiming its rightful property.

The Italian architect took his own life soon after the money ran out upon construction of the outer shell; his brainchild stillborn. The interior was never completed. Well, not by Franco Belfi. Caoin invited me inside.

○

Ironically, shared spaces had sashayed into vogue of late. Whether for working or living or more likely both as what's the fucking difference, there was no shortage of applicants willing or resigned to piling in together and middlemen keen to facilitate the trend. Far as I knew, none of the attempts to fabricate cohabitation in the region during its most recent false dawn had got anywhere near to realisation before losses were cut. Doubt the collective that had occupied the old blueprint

I was sauntering through were the class of clientele that modern developers were looking to attract.

Whatever the ultimate vision for the nucleus of the Molecule had been, the basic form, fashioned from the same tough stuff as the facade, was astonishingly circular and smooth. At a quick count, twenty-four small uniform rooms ran the circumference of an upper-level balcony. Directly below them, the outskirts of the communal area were divided into two chambers and two recesses, each with a specific purpose.

Most immediately eye-catching was the kitchen, a glaring concoction of scavenged catering equipment. The stainless steal pieces didn't fit together seamlessly and were hardly homely, but were a practical choice for the circumstances.

A cold store, evidenced by the white wisps seeping around the edges of its bulky hatch, was mirrored by a washroom, downbeat trip hop that could have been made yesterday or decades ago echoing around its sterile surfaces. The sound of the occupant — or perhaps plural — shifting under the splattering shower was the nearest thing to a confirmed sign of life in the place. Assumed most of the residents were still out in the field, but there were a few lights spilling around the edges of doorways and muffled multilingual conversations mingling in the ether.

The focal point of the panopticon was designated primarily for dining and meeting, with a patchwork of tables slotted like tetronimoes into an uneven slab big enough to accommodate all at once, surrounded by an appropriately eclectic gaggle of chairs. The scattering of soft furnishings were of equally diverse provenance as were the fixtures and fittings. Shouldn't have worked but it really kind of did. Rough around the edges sure, but it had organically become something not far off what an on-trend design firm would do for a large consultancy fee; casual cosiness mixed with textural bite to give that urban rustic aesthetic so many go out of their way to achieve.

The final quadrant was a library of sorts, with densely packed books forming their own shelves. Had little chance to peruse but it looked to contain more hefty texts than light reading. Right on cue, a retro payphone that I hadn't registered, held in place at the centre possibly by the weight of words alone, started to ring. Couldn't remember the last time I even saw a coin outside a dusty jar by my front door if you actually had to feed the thing to call out. No one rushed to answer the shrill warble. Certainly not Caoin — had other things on her mind as we entered the stairwell.

XV

"What were you looking for?"

Caoin swivelled on her heels before I could work out quite what she was asking, somewhat forcibly stopping me mid-way up the swirling ramp to the next level. The steep curve made us the same height and the ridges of my ribcage fit her delicate hand like a glove. She kept it there and my expectations at a half-arm's length while checking me out.

"I mean, whatever led you all the way down through the Ashes to me?"

In hindsight it was harmless enough — trying to figure if I'd been hunting an elusive creature such as herself or was just lucky. Both were true. But my reading of the question was overridden by an uneasy feeling, like being caught hiding.

"Jack?"

Fuck. That dragged my disquiet out into the open. All that had happened between me and her was sincere but couldn't deny to myself I'd got lost in the role I'd been playing, pretending to be something I wasn't. Could have levelled then; who I really was and what brought me there that night. Should have.

I'd quick become accustomed to the period of grace she gave for a natural response and it had already passed. Knew what was coming next. No time to debate if the only move I could think of was the correct one. Same instant she leant forward I did too but twice the distance, pressing the very corner of my mouth against hers as our cheeks brushed.

Might have come across like I bottled at the last moment or just outright missed but it landed as intended, a forward gesture that I hoped wouldn't be overly offensive if it turned out to be misjudged. She pulled back, blushing just as quick, her gaze falling away a heartbeat later. She remained still and I did the same. Her fingertips grazed down my midriff, gripping the stitching of my jean pocket to slide herself close. Holding me in place solely with the return of her glistening eyes she delved deeper, promptly finding the only thing other than her number I had in there.

"Oh... what have we here?"

All but forgotten since that morning, she presented the scavenged pearl between her middle and ring fingers.

"Where'd you get this?" she demanded in an arch authoritative tone.

"Found it," I coyly played along.

"That old story. Well I'm not buying. Furthermore, I don't believe you just stumbled into my world. I know what you were really looking for."

"Yeah?"

"Aye. Trouble."

The capsule popped open with a flick of the wrist that suggested she'd done it at least a handful of times before. She dipped a pinky into the viscous narcotic then dabbed the tip of her tongue, letting it settle a second before licking her lips.

"Found that too, I'd say."

The empty canister clinked to the ground and rolled away. She grabbed me by the scruff of the neck, the warmth of the kiss chased by a cold trickle into my chest.

○

The room was dark. Pitch black in fact.

I'd already lost sight of Caoin as she stole around the edge of a heavy textile sheet, hanging in place of a door above the threshold of her quarters. Following her in I found myself faced with a second curtain hung from the other side. Couldn't see anything between the two and even less once I'd swept through.

I knew where she was, a few steps ahead. Following her soft distinct scent, I glided along the current of heat she'd left behind. Heard the zip and flop of her hoodie being discarded, my jacket close behind it. Toes of my boots found the bed, no time to take them off. I folded down to the mattress, low on the floor.

Her breathing drew me in. Waiting faced away from me, I slid in close behind, the palm of my hand resting on the pyramid of her hip. I nuzzled the nape of her neck, kissing the central groove and round to the right angle of her jaw, then her ear, her cheek. She turned her head so our lips could meet, a significant moment before they parted. I wanted to know every minutia of her face, continuing up to the bridge of her nose, an eyelid, the corner of a brow.

Burying her face into the pillow she took my hand, brushing it between her legs and up over the feminine swell of her stomach. She chose not to wear a bra, her breasts small and firm, set back from her ribs the way her frame was arched. My hand was only allowed there a second before being guided to her outstretched throat. I gripped it lightly.

She threw her arm back, tangling it under mine and grabbing my crotch hard through my jeans. I kissed her shoulders, teething aside a kinked strip of fabric as I made my way across. Her hand moved around to my back, leveraging herself even closer before snaking up to rejoin mine. We twined fingers in different formations, finding one that fit perfect, my arm wrapped around her. We rocked gently. I couldn't hold her tight enough.

She let out a little moan, pushing against me subtly but with clear intent. I traced my palm along the crook of her arm and back to the hip, pausing there until she gave me another nudge, more insistent. My hand plunged down her leg to find the hem of her dress, peeling up half the fringe. I grazed my nails back down the outside of her thigh, working my fingers in to cup her knee then sliding my hand up the inside, feeling the moisture before the cotton. She opened a fraction so I could slip underneath, holding her between thumb and forefinger. She rubbed against my hand then jolted back into me with an assertive grunt. I reached around for a handful of her curves, more pert than her slim figure had led me to believe.

I pushed her away a couple inches. While I undid my belt and popped open the row of buttons, she snatched the rest of her skirt out from under her then groped around to grasp all of me through my briefs before wrestling the waistband over the top. Pressing back against her I discovered her knickers had disappeared too, both of us stunned by the feel of the intimacy. She gasped as I didn't hesitate any longer.

From there we took it slow. I didn't dare go too fast too soon. Little by little, focusing on her responses, I moved steadily further in, picking up the pace until she suddenly rolled me onto my back. She didn't weigh a thing.

Girl could really move, twisting in whatever direction felt right to her. Felt right to me too. Straps slipped to her elbows as I pulled down the front of her dress and held her against me. Clasping her nipples took her to the edge, near enough pushing her over when I continued down to caress her natural shock of hair.

Hurrying up to our knees, I ripped the collar of my tee tearing it off. Jeans around my thighs, her dress a narrow band around her midriff, I grabbed her all in by the waist. Though we were going hard and heavy, I witnessed my fingertips tracing tenderly over a full-grown pair of resting wings, ever so faint. Tattoo must have been fresh. Then I got a strange sensation they were fluttering, just slightly, in time with her quickening exhalations.

She pulled away and flipped onto her back, grabbing me by the shoulders with both hands and pulling me down. Such was our rush we stumbled to find each other, both groaning loudly when our bones clattered. Other than that outburst all our non-physical dialogue had been breathless sighs and primal growls, but then, locked from ankles to wrists, faces side by side, there was something else — something deeper. Her mouth was right next to my ear but I know she wasn't talking. Could hear her inside my head. Or rather throughout my body. More expressive than words could be, saying so much but most of all that it was time.

I was ready too. Started to move with purpose and her hands came away from mine and fell to her side, her whole form rigid. I kept the flow steady and strong; committed, no backing out. After shuddering like a surge of energy had rippled right through her, ten nails dug into my lower back, slowly climbing my spine until we had nothing left to give.

...

What's the time?

First thought. Always. Racing against myself to fall back inside the lines, seeking orientation outside my senses.

Is that a breeze?

Drifting through the night, a straight road all the way home, found myself at a dead end. Would usually collapse when I couldn't progress any further, not solely down to irredeemable fractures in narrative or logic or tolerance, could be something innocuous as trying to read or write or tell the...

This time was different, recognised where I was. Announced to the world I'd figured it out and had decided to fly. Right there and then. Took off. To an extent. Couldn't soar beyond that mental cul-de-sac, but was able to swoop and glide within. That's when I woke up. Wondering if I was lucid dreaming or just dreaming I was lucid dreaming.

Are my eyes open or closed?

Can't see anything. Must be open. At best can view a few miles out — no limits in. Distance, direction, dimension. Now appears just as dark, empty, but it's there. Everything. Couldn't all belong to me, impossibly vast. I feel separate, a singular fragment, observing. Unable to see myself, no looking inwards from here. Harder I try, smaller I become, a lone speck of consciousness in an infinite void.

Water. I need water...

XVI

Raining again. Not quite what I had in mind.

Sounded heavy, filling the space deserted by light. The breeze stroked my skin, placing the pieces of my body, putting it back together. Lying flat on my back, I tried to count some deep breaths — six in, six out — but there was a discord between what I could feel and hear. Discerned the quicker, shallower rhythm I'd been listening to wasn't my own. Caoin was fast asleep somewhere by my side. Didn't want to disturb her so resisted the instinct to reach out.

Raising onto my elbows I stabbed myself in the stomach; still rock hard. Shimmied my jeans back around my waist, tucking in as best I could. Force of habit shoved a hand into my pocket, rummaging around in discomfort before I remembered something had happened to my phone. Knew an answer of sorts to the first question I would have asked of it anyway — was time to get up.

Once on my feet the lack of sight as an available sense became more problematic. Remembering how I'd come in, I located the edges of the mattress with prods of my boots then turned one-eighty and walked straight, reaching out until I'd gathered a handful of fabric. Peeling it aside revealed not another curtain as expected but a figure stood in front of me, dark and undefined. I was too spooked to move. They were just as still. Watched myself slowly reaching out. They reached out too. Our hands met and I felt the cold touch of the frosted window.

Palm to palm with a muted approximation of my image, I trailed a blurred edge down the thick glass bricks, nails finding a path of crumbling mortar that led to the entrance of the spirited little wind. Cupping the satisfyingly convex bulk of a loose slab near the centre, it budged backwards and I pulled away short of pushing it out the other side.

Leaving a large triangle of moonlight streaming in, I tucked half the blind over an ornament fixed to the wall, which I recall remarkably clearly as an anthropomorphised rabbit in a hunting jacket with curling horns for legs. Glimpsing the room for the first time it seemed back to front to my imagination — either it had got completely turned around or we did.

Caoin looked at peace, on her side in a foetal ball. Strangest thing, I couldn't see a tattoo anywhere on her body. Her modesty was almost back intact of its own accord but I gave it a little help, delicately moving her straps into position as appropriate and wrapping the hem of her dress around her curled-up knees. While down there I brushed a stray curl behind her ear and kissed her softly on the temple. She shivered a little as I pulled away. We had been on top of the blanket the entire time and after a moment weighing up how to get her under, I settled on the solution of folding the other half on top.

My T-shirt was at the foot of the mattress and I ripped the neck a little more grappling it over my head. Didn't do much against the chill that had really started to take a hold. Handily, my jacket wrapped around my feet as I dragged them across the floor. Grabbing it by the arm holes and flipping it on in one smooth motion left me defenceless to a bash on the hip from something solid that I missed protruding from the wall. The vintage sink wasn't the answer to my immediate need however, the tap bone dry. I continued to the doorway and a brief tangle with the double blackouts.

○

Took the scenic route to the stairwell. Unintentionally. Had shuffled more than half-way around the balcony before twigging I'd turned the wrong direction. The fluorescent strips overhead, all too easy to ignore before, had become a domineering presence. Couldn't hear much over the heavens lashing the skylights but there didn't seem to be a peep from any of the rooms. Though some had more personalised fabrics in place of doors, from well-travelled rugs to sheer sheets of linen that looked pretty and offered little in the way of privacy, most had the same utilitarian black textile. Wished I made a better mental note of which one was Caoin's.

The vortex to the ground floor was almost too much to handle. Or rather, I needed something that I actually could handle. Resolved the best way to traverse it was to lean my back against the wall, stretch out my arms, and essentially slither down. Not the most dignified form of movement but thankfully no one was there to see it.

Glad as I was not having to make small talk, the cavernous echo of my footsteps across the living space amplified a feeling of being unnaturally alone, as if I was that character who wakes up into the apocalypse. The kitchen tap was a robust work of apparatus, a thick pipe stretching up three feet before curving around and becoming a hose hanging all the way back down. Couldn't immediately see how to turn it on, startling myself with the jet that shot out when I fumbled the business end. Leaning over the sink I brought the nozzle to my head and squeezed the handheld trigger. Water never tasted so good. I drank ceaselessly for at least a minute, washing away the metallic tang, only stopping when the ringing started.

Call it prying, with no small measure of self-absorption mixed in, but whenever I saw a stray letter or package, pretty much anywhere, I'd check the label. Not under the presumption it could be for me of course, rather a compulsion to involve myself in its unfinished story. Was the same kind of thought process that had me heading for the payphone.

Feeling progressively human with each step, it still took me long enough to slouch over there that I'd fully reasoned it was none of my business, and guessed the secondary question of whether I was about to answer it anyhow would be taken out of my hands when it would abruptly stop. Surely any second. But it carried on and so did I, my hand reaching for the cracked back of the receiver when the strangled chime choked and died.

My arm kept going though, slowly and upwards. While my immediate attention had become consumed by the intricate spectacle of the curved wall of books, hypnotised by the warp and weft of interlocking spines, a more intuitive part of my brain was cutting to the chase. It was right in my eye line but my fingertips found it first — stood amongst a vertical row was a chunk of yellow plastic. I pulled it out and the retro walkman's earphones trailed after it, swinging in the air like a noose. The familiarity of the object and the unexpected intersection of my pursuits brought no comfort. Quite the opposite.

I reined in the flexy metal headband and popped on the foam pads. Examining the veteran piece of hardware, I couldn't tell through the little window if there was a tape inside. Was years since I'd handled it myself and rather than flip open the catch that enclosed the buttons and held the flap shut, muscle memory took my thumb straight to the pleasing thunk of play. By the day's standard it was slow to start — a fraction of a second, but noticeable when you're used to instant everything. Didn't take much longer than that before I ripped them off my head, a reflex to the top volume skreigh straight into my ear. Was just as shocking to see the cause of the noise staring at me from across the room.

Vanda remained still as a statue. Most obvious thing off about her was the missing track top, especially considering the beating she'd taken from the storm.

Naturally concerned by her shellshocked appearance, I was distracted from the reels still whirring in my hand, headphones tailing behind me like a collar that had lost its dog as I cautiously approached.

"You okay?"

She didn't answer, but more clues emerged the closer I got. Could see her chest pumping, efforts to regain control of her breathing hampered by the fact she didn't want to let it show. Little rivers ran the contours of her bare skin, rushing down her arms and dripping onto the floor by way of her bloodied knuckles.

"What happened?"

"Well," she finally spoke with breath just about caught, "they got the message."

She backed to the sink, studying her fists. I took that as a sign I was close enough and stopped by the communal table. She didn't wince when she blasted each hand in turn with the tap, probably masking any urge she may have had to.

Repositioning to forty-five degrees so as not to leave her flank totally exposed, she bent over and cupped some water into her mouth. Her top was heavily marked and stretched near the waist, as if a handful had been grabbed of it. Her pant leg on the opposite side flared loose from her boot, torn to the back of the knee;

snagged while haring through the woods I reckoned. A tuft of her previously tight-bound hair shone in the harsh light. She palmed it slick as she straightened tall.

"Didn't go down so smooth," she followed up, facing me again. "Turned into this whole... big thing."

Then she heard it, the tinny reproduction of her voice playing from somewhere. Finding the source by my feet, she traced the wire up to the tired old machine in my hand. I saw her mind tick; reliving the past, contemplating possible futures and how the person standing opposite might fit into both — or not. I saw her face betray her default stoicism, revealing a rush of uncertainty before recomposing. And she saw that I saw.

"Where did this come from?" I asked in a solemn tone.

She looked away, shifting her weight to one foot, about to put the expanse of the table between us. I intercepted the movement by sliding the walkman across the patchwork surface into her path. She caught the falling body one-handed as it skidded off the edge, regarding it soberly before hitting the stop button.

"I knew there was something about you," she sighed, winding up the slack rubber strands.

Rocking back onto the other foot, she padded towards me, still avoiding eye contact.

"It's not what you think."

"Tell me," I pressed on.

Six feet away she placed the walkman down precisely then looked up sharply.

"We really liked Kofi."

Everything went black — only for an instant before my eyes started adjusting to the four-foot-square moonbeams from the streaking skylights, one splitting Vanda straight down the middle.

"Fuck," she whispered."

"Where is he?" I demanded undeterred.

"Fuck, fuck, fuck..."

"Hey!" I snapped, "where... is..."

"You don't understand," her intensity rose, "this isn't right."

"Quit stalling, it's just another cut."

"No. We have our own power, out back..."

Tough to say exactly which of two things happened next, the staggering crunch of the main doors being breached or Vanda getting low and moving fast. Caught glimpses as she passed through the shafts before I lost her. Then I picked up more footsteps, heavier. Trying to track multiple flashes of motion I didn't see it coming, a push as much as a grab of my open jacket collar, slamming me against the edge of the table. A dark figure leaned in close. Too close — my face pressed hard against the steamed-up perspex of a riot helmet.

XVII

Blacklock made quite the first impression.

Forcefully harried into the driving rain through two lines of officers forming a tunnel either side the buckled doors, body-mounted flashlights glaring through scuffed three-quarter-length shields, I was slung to a designated patch of ground, a gloved fist brandishing linked zip-ties signalling me to stay right there. Path of least resistance had kept my wrists free, full compliance marking me down as low threat, and it was in my interests the assessment stayed that way. While avoiding the limits that being trussed up would impose on my options was the main objective, I also doubted liberal use of the baton in my captor's other hand required much provocation. Making a break for it would certainly qualify.

Wouldn't usually contemplate running from the police. Sure I had in the past, when the circumstances demanded it, but for the most part I'd lived the right side of the law, and even when I was unduly targeted my societal profile meant I had a high chance of walking away if I played it straight. On this occasion though

I couldn't rely on that passive defence. Activism and anarchy had long been present in the hippie communes that gave birth to the punk houses, but an unmeasured dose of nihilism had been injected into the mix during or causing the mutation to industrial collectives. For all I might now be guilty of by association however, the more pressing concern was that these were not real police.

Granted they looked the part, if a touch too well equipped; private contractor status awarding unrestricted budgets and access to the surplus catalogues of hardcore enforcement agencies. Fortunately, firearms were still not yet widespread, but most sported the latest in the line of tasers clipped to their hips. All-black uniforms, cut from dynamic composites, pinched and puffed in the right places. The reinforced elements were distinctly sculpted, from the boots, pads, chest plates to most notably the helmets — everything had a futuristic bent, diminishing the humanity. Had to remind myself that in addition to function, this kind of gear was designed to invoke fear, strike a blow before the battle had begun. Underneath it all they were just men.

That was what really worried me. I didn't trust the traditional authorities much but this firm was far less accountable. Aggressive reaction as a default mode would explain why I'd never witnessed them as a preventative presence before, but regardless of policy, when a mob rolls out with pitchforks the outcome is practically set in stone. Whether the operation I'd been caught up in was a long time coming or simply extended from what I could only presume was a heavy-handed dispersal of that forbidden gathering, how civil the current situation remained depended largely on the compassion of these faceless figures.

Not saying every one of them was a thug; while the majority would have actively sought out such mercenary work, some would have had little other opportunity to earn a living. Still I assumed the worst, or at best indifference, from a militant unit repeatedly drilled with a volatile warrior mindset by a fundamentally corrupt institution.

A commotion at the entrance soon confirmed my suspicions. Sticks and kicks pelted a noncompliant as they were paraded through the guard of honour. Despite a deep relief that I didn't recognise the limp body discarded by a four-spot squad before they headed back in, I felt sick to the stomach at the sight of the middle-aged man's scrawny crumpled form.

With codes of conduct flying out the window so was I — the thought solidifying in my head as when, not if,

155

I made a move. While discreetly considering my personal sentry, the dozen by the door and the handful inside, I also had to factor in the austere rays reaching through the trees. Their vehicles could only get so close but they no doubt had some level of back-up standing by there too. Unless I ran straight in their direction they wouldn't figure in any chase, just hoped they didn't have dogs.

Getting ahead of myself though. Make it into the woods and there's no way those in the vicinity could keep up bulked down in all that kit. Realised my guard was distractedly watching the same drone I'd seen in the field before, now circling the building. Hadn't counted on evading a mechanical raptor but nevertheless this represented the best chance I had to flee. Of course it was never that simple — I had no intention of escaping alone.

There were two curious things about the way the rain stopped. Firstly, it was near instant, like turning off a shower. Secondly, the disappearance of the white noise revealed it had been masking another sound, growing loud. Soon, the incoming clamour had got inside the helmets, rattling their composure. They didn't seem so much like robots, the formation at the door losing rigidity, previously stiff stances becoming apprehensive as they tried to make sense of the dozens of tiny lights moving erratically fast amongst the forest.

Half the unit had already backed inside by time a familiar but much more powerful war cry became clear, the rest turning tail as the spearhead of the cavalry pierced the tree line — Blacklock weren't the only ones that had rocked up for the afterparty. Last holdout was my sentry, his retreat delayed as he paused to take a wild swing at me with his hi-tech club. An instinctive limbo that left me on my back was the only thing that saved my skull.

From there I watched them rushing past, torches and phone screens spotlighting the rage on the faces I'd ran and raved alongside. Hands reached underneath me, supporting my frame as I was whisked up and into the storm for the entrance — my would-be attacker hadn't made it in.

O

Chaos. Fucking chaos.

The hectic sights and frenzied sounds of the battle were more jarring than anything I'd come across that night. Blacklock had been scattered by the time I got back in the building, an attempt to form a chokepoint at the double doors not holding out long against the sheer weight of numbers. Drawing the most attention, a core of half-a-dozen had taken an elevated stand on the central tables, shields and truncheons maintaining a perimeter against the swarms attacking head on and from beneath, all the while being pelted with kitchen sundries. Flashes and crackles of tasers from both the cold store and shower room highlighted the desperate skirmishes within. Meanwhile, a tight line of four were edging as yet unchallenged across the living space.

Had no interest in engaging with any of them but knew I had to beat the retreating unit to the stairwell. With a crowd massed in front, the clash imminent, I bobbed and weaved at top speed around the periphery, wide enough to avoid contact. As I raced towards the foot of the ramp, an isolated officer stumbled down it, moving to intercept. He was off balance when I threw my shoulder and everything I had against his shield, slamming him into the wall of books. I hardly broke stride as he was buried by the collapse.

Tore up the bend so fast I didn't register the pain down my whole right side until I'd reached the top. Went the correct direction without even thinking, systematically sweeping open each black curtain in turn. Two down, no joy, I glanced at a sheet of crimson linen as I passed and saw a shadow growing behind it. That fraction of warning before the officer burst out meant I managed to sidestep an overhead chop, so heavy the rod smashed a chunk out of the guardrail. I recoiled from his swinging advance until he stopped and dropped the baton, drawing his taser. As he lined me up, a bear of a man charged blindly through a hanging Afghan rug, tackling the officer straight over the balcony and toppling his confederates holding fort on the table below. Didn't spare a second to see what happened after the splat, just kept moving.

Next black sheet revealed another behind it. I swam through into the triangle of moonlight I'd left in the room. Hurrying to the bed I whipped away the blanket — Caoin had gone. My eyes darted over every inch three times before I accepted she was no longer in there. I felt a cold chill, literally. Moving to the window I examined a quick-and-dirty opening that had been excavated in the glass bricks, large enough to fit a small person.

I shoved and grabbed at the edges, expanding the hole. A whoosh of fabric and stomping of boots spun me on my heels. Luckily the officer had entered backwards, guarding the doorway. Brick already in hand, I wound up and pitched it straight at a sweet spot above the belt and below the body armour. He keeled over instantly. Not knowing how long he'd be incapacitated hastened me out onto the ledge.

The box that housed the window was a good couple feet wide but it was a long way down. Peeking around the edge I could see potential routes across the other protrusions. Didn't have much choice anyway. Turning my back to the drop, I planted my palms on top the flat surface above and lifted myself up as if my life depended on it. Which it did.

From there I hurriedly plotted a course: a lunge down onto the neighbouring window block; short hop to a diagonal concrete dash leading to a series of dots climbing higher than my starting point; big jump to land on a vent; pull up to the roof. Easy. Just had to actually do it.

The very first step, taken without delay, brought me crashing back to reality. Almost doing the splits as my foot skidded in a thin coat of rainwater collected on the adjacent platform left me feeling hollow at what could have been. This wasn't a game. I gathered my composure then visualised the next move twice before making it.

By the end of the dash, uncertainty in my plan was increasing, no matter how methodically I was enacting it. Steadying myself with a hand against the wall I stepped to the first dot and paused; second, paused; third I found to be uneven, weather-beaten to roughly the size and shape of my foot. Wouldn't suffice as a staging post before the riskiest link in the chain. Only way it would work was to fluidly advance. All or nothing.

I reversed my steps back to the dash and mentally double-checked my footwork, needing to make sure I led off from the last dot with my inside leg. The dissonance inside me was physically palpable, one force pushing, another restraining, until in a terrifying instant I was doing it — one, two, three...

I landed on top of the vent with air to spare, nearly clearing the whole thing. Taking a moment to look back over the mountain I'd scaled revealed that had I known there was an alcove directly under Caoin's window, I could have lowered myself into it and taken an easier path down to the ground. The prospect of going back was even worse than what I'd just done. Didn't rue it long. The screech and snap of old metal giving way to my weight had me scrabbling up onto the roof as the casing ripped from the wall and plummeted.

A few steps across the top of the building, I was reminded of the fierce conflict below by a cluster of booms, disorientating even all the way up there. Peering through a skylight I saw tear gas spiking the air along with another score of Blacklock troops piling in.

I scurried to the opposite corner, searching for a

place to start a descent as far from the doors as possible. Had plotted a whole route before I spotted I wasn't alone — the drone hovering eerily still a few feet away. Couldn't tell if it was looking straight at me or out over the woods, if front and back even applied to such a thing. It didn't react when I slowly reached for the rusted piping jutting out by my feet and wrenched it loose. Nor when I raised the length over my head. First hit brought the machine crashing to the roof where it buzzed and spasmed until a second bash put it out of its misery. Guess it wasn't looking at me.

Then I saw what it had been watching, a slight figure escaping through the trees. Maybe it wasn't Caoin, just seeing what I wanted to see, but was all I had to go on.

XVIII

Running towards trouble was fast becoming a habit.

Only clear sign I wasn't chasing a ghost through the trees were the lights I headed straight for strobing as something tangible crossed them. The beams grew rapidly in intensity, as if they were bearing down, until I was suddenly out of the woods and into the glare of eight Blacklock *meat wagons*, clustered at the dead-end clearing of a rough trail. The vehicles appeared to have been hastily evacuated, doors left flung open. Even so, I would have gone nowhere near them if that had been an option, but the margins were narrow due to the sheer bank to my left and the rocky outcrop to my right, the sea thrashing far below.

Proceeding with caution proved to be the right decision. Approaching the first van a gunshot thumped, echoes swirling in the stiff wind. I fell to my stomach and put an ear to the ground, using the small gap between front tyre and bumper to survey the area. No sign of movement until a silhouette hurtled from behind one wagon to the next, just in time to evade a tracking blast. From the damage left on the metal hull it struck, denting rather than shredding, I figured on rubber bullets. Some relief, but still didn't want to get in the way of one.

Crawling under the axle I heard another hustle of feet and another two shots, the game of cat and mouse escalating. Coast clear, I emerged and bounded into the passenger side of the next van, clambering across the cab and out the driver's door to shimmy along its length between the bank.

Pressed against the metal edge I could just about spy the shooter — crouched between a pair of splayed back doors, aim trained on the final bulk of four-wheeled cover before the path stretched up and away. I waited as he waited.

The shadow made her move and so did I. First shot flew wide; second bouncing off the ground near her feet as she broke into the clear. Third hit her square in the shoulder, spinning Vanda full circle before she righted herself and ran on. The shooter racked but didn't rush, thinking he could afford to make the last shot count, so zeroed he never knew I was inbound. With the force of a twenty foot run-up I kicked the van door into him, shotgun going off sideways as he was sandwiched against the tailgate.

The officer was pretty out of it when I fronted him

up. Glasses smashed and not decked out in tactical gear like the rest, I took him for a drone operator with idle hands judging from the bank of blank monitors in the back of his vehicle. I slammed him with the other door to be sure before I took off in pursuit.

○

Always more a sprinter than a distance runner in my school days. Not the very fastest but one of them, a solid third leg in the relay. Still had much of that propulsive snap, the twitch reflex for a sudden burst, but sustaining it over a hundred metres no longer came so naturally. Compensating for this shortfall, I'd developed something that experience had taught me to appreciate just as much — stamina.

Had to catch Vanda. Not only was she the best chance I had of seeing Caoin again but we also had to finish what we started in the kitchen before the night caught fire. She knew something about Kofi and I was going to know it too.

Outlook from the start was not good; my boots sliding in the gravel, thighs burning from the incline, the air plentiful but somehow abrasive to my lungs. In contrast Vanda looked like she could run a marathon, pulling briskly away. I kept going. Steady. Driven.

Higher we climbed. Couldn't tell it from her form — head and back straight, arms and legs pumping — but she was definitely lagging. We had both been through excessive exertions but she was feeling the effects most in that moment. Knew this because I was gaining by the second.

She clocked on I was there, glancing over her shoulder that I was so close to I could see the rubber bullet's point of impact and the bruise radiating around it. Nearing the peak of the trail, a dangerous curve with the bank high and sharp one side, the craggy buffer to a fatal fall at its flattest and narrowest the other, she found an extra gear, a sprint finish giving her the space to slide to a halt and face me, fists clenched tight but held low near her waist.

"Stop!" she screeched and I did, soon as momentum would allow.

"Just wanna know what happened to Kofi," I said calmly as I could, palms open and high.

"You don't," she told me in a tone as firm as her stance, "pulling at that tail will get you bit. Let it go."

The wind whipped around us. She wasn't about to budge but neither was I.

"Gonna have to say more than that to convince me."

She scowled. "What are you, some kind of fucking hero?"

"No," I lowered my head. "An old friend."

"Okay," she relaxed her frame a shade, "okay. It was the girl."

"Caoin?"

"Met him at a record store, he was buying one of my tapes. Got chatting, invited him to a show at the Ashes. Nice guy, but really she was looking for customers."

"What kind of customers?" I queried, my unease increasing as Vanda paced sideways, compelling me to mirror her arcing trajectory.

"Pearls," was uttered under her breath.

"She slings?"

"All gotta pay our way," sounded like a proclamation she'd made before.

"But Kofi... he was diving?"

A firm shake of the head dismissed the suspicion.

"Didn't even seem to swim. Kay gave him a free sample and he kept coming to nights but never bought anything. More into the music. More into me," she added matter of factly.

"Guess the feeling wasn't mutual."

"Not my type," she smiled, "but I took a shine to him, we both did. Kept following our shows and came back with us one night. Loved the place, wanted to move on in."

"And?" I urged her forward as Vanda abruptly reversed the direction of her strafing, causing me to do the same.

"We said why not, had a room going. He was so happy. Wanted to do something special to mark the date, taste a pearl. Kay let him have another on the house. Checked on him next morning and he was gone."

"Gone?"

"Gone. Overdose. Wouldn't have felt a thing."

I went numb as the revelation crept through me. I all but knew he was dead from the moment she had first used his name in the past tense, yet hearing it spelled out made it seem like it had just happened.

"How many did he do?"

She answered by holding up a single finger, also signalling the end of our slow dance. Didn't pass me by that our circling had ended with my back to the drop.

"Must have been tainted," she elaborated. "Maybe if he hadn't taken the whole thing he... no, it can't be changed. A bad batch can get caught up in the mix."

I'd perused a few long-read horror stories on the subject; lab quality control rejects or straight-up bootlegs dripping onto the streets every blue moon.

Tiny discrepancy in the chemical concentration meant a world of difference.

"Where did she get them from?"

Vanda bit the tip of her tongue, toying with her phrasing before sharing it. "I make sure everybody gets what they need."

"Or more than they bargained for," I simmered.

"Luck of the spin," she reasoned, "fucking roulette. Had to toss the whole stash into the sea."

"What did you do with Kofi?" I was hesitant to ask.

Her eyes gave it away, at pains to avoid looking out over the water.

"You could have left him somewhere he'd be found," I seethed, close to boiling point.

"No one else needed be involved," she coldly asserted.

Done with it all, I took a diagonal step down the trail but Vanda moved into my path.

"Where are you going?" she demanded.

"To find Caoin, make sure she's safe," I answered, trying to proceed but stopped by a hand to my chest.

"And then?"

"Then I'm going to see Kofi's mother."

I tried to push on but the hand pushed back.

"To say what exactly?"

"Nothing more than necessary. But she's waiting for him to come home, needs to hear something."

"All I've told you is not enough to change your mind?"

I brushed her hand aside and it landed on my shoulder.

"Wait, listen..."

I gave her one more moment.

"Would you want to know?" she asked sincerely.

"What do you mean?"

"Think on it. There's always a chance he's still out there somewhere until she knows for sure he's not. Is the truth really what's right for her or what's right for you?"

She had cut straight to the heart of the matter, giving me pause for serious thought. Maybe the reason I was so fixed on bringing Kofi home, even if in words only, was because I had never been able to do the same for Maddison — explain why he was serving life because in desperation I'd played his strong sense of loyalty and weak grip on reality to save my own skin when the past had come calling. There and then I decided, *promised*, that after I'd delivered the bad news to Val I'd also reveal what really went down that night. But for anyone to ever hear that story I first had to be alive to Vanda's gambit.

She threw a low hooking right at my ribs and it was pure reflex that caught her wrist with my left. She didn't pull it away, instead trying to force her fist towards me despite the lack of momentum, locking her legs and hold on my shoulder for extra purchase. Recognising her intention with alarm, I juked my hip to avoid the bulk of the switchblade concealed inside her mitt from opening straight into me. Puncture it made in my side was no more than half an inch deep and wide but felt like a heavyweight body blow.

I grabbed her above the elbow with my right and cranked her arm back. She let it go loose and our limbs swung between the middle of us, the blade scarcely missing my stomach. Releasing her other hand from my shoulder, she swapped the knife into it, the cock that preceded the thrust giving me a split-second to transfer my grip, latching on to prevent being skewered. She wrapped her free fingers stiffly around my wrist closest to the point of action, leveraging my own body against me while tying us up in a figure of eight.

Fit as Vanda was, she wouldn't have been able to overpower me if not for the damage I'd done throwing myself at a riot shield, really starting to make itself known. She retracted the blade as it came near, removing any certainty I had of the striking distance.

With little else in the way of options, I slid a hand up her arm and clutched her bruised shoulder tight as I could. She yelped, dropping the knife, before sinking her teeth around my wrist bone. Not proud of this, should never hit a woman, but in an instant I'd angled her to face me and planted my forehead hard between her eyes.

She stumbled, hand to her nose. Peeling it away, she glared at the blood pooling in her palm then looked up with the most savage daggers I'd ever seen. She scraped a forearm across her mouth. I readied myself for the next assault but wasn't prepared for how it came. Shaking with wrath, like she could barely contain herself, she stamped forward and roared with such a sustained and piercing fury that it repelled me backwards. Just a step. Wind and the wet rock did the rest.

○

For what felt like a lifetime there was nothing beneath me but the waiting sea.

In actuality it was less than a heartbeat before my torso had clattered against the edge of the drop, frantic grasping lucking into a jagged crevice with one hand and onto a slippery bulge with the other. Legs flailing against the cliff face, my whole weight was in my fingertips for an excruciating second until my feet settled precariously on a ridge no deeper than my big toe.

Every thread of my body was screaming, almost as loud as the fracas within. I tried to focus on the calmest voice, the one saying just hold on, but it was quickly drowned out by all the others arguing that climbing up unaided was impossible and it was only a matter of time before I fell.

Vanda wasn't willing to wait that long. Crouching at the precipice, she slid a foot down the steep slope to where everything became vertical and my hand clung desperately atop the slick swell. Soon judging the move to be too much risk, she retracted and crawled away.

Returning with knife in hand, her first thought was to hurl it at me, even starting the motion, before shifting to a more certain solution. Finding a suitable crack by her feet she jammed the blade in, gripping the handle as she lowered a leg. Slithering closer, she rested her sole on my fingers a moment before winding up and stamping down hard, the shock of pain such that I might have reflexively let go if my hand hadn't been stuck between her foot and the rock. Seeing the flaw in her technique, she took a probing scuff across my snow white knuckles. My grip was waning. She wound up again, angling to deliver the mix of power and accuracy that would finish me off. She let fly but the kick fell short as she was dragged backwards.

"Fuck are you doing?" I heard Caoin yell before she peered over at me. "Jesus!"

Caoin dropped to her knees and reached out. Didn't have a chance to reach back before Vanda pulled her to her feet.

"He has to go," Vanda snapped.

"What the hell, Vee? Why?" Caoin shrieked in her face, only getting half-way down to me before she was stood up straight again and held by her wriggling shoulders.

"He's not who he says he is," Vanda hissed, turning Caoin's face back when she tried to look at me. "He came in search of Kofi."

Caoin stopped struggling.

"What..."

"Some friend of the family's, he'll tell everything."

Caoin glanced at me then away just as quick. One of my feet came loose, pulling my hand from the crevice after it. Nails scraped down rock before my forefingers found a home in a brace of rough holes and my toes nestled into a solid groove a few inches below the ridge. My elbow was locked to my hip, pressing against the stab wound, and the other side of my body, already weakened, was far overstretched. No strain on my muscles, they no longer seemed to exist, the pain concentrated in my bones. The bittersweet thing — felt I could hold myself there but had no strength to move.

Caoin paced with her hands clasped behind her head.

"Maybe we should," she exhaled when she'd circled around.

"Should what?" Vanda practically spat, already rejecting the answer.

"Tell. Everything. Like I wanted to in the first place."

"That place is no more. As is our home. We can run, hide, find somewhere to build a new one, but not if we have a dead body trailing after us..."

"Two bodies!" Caoin bawled, pointing at me.

"And then who will know? It's simple, his life for the both of ours."

Caoin shook her head.

"This shouldn't be happening. It was an accident."

"Yes. It was not your fault. Neither is this."

Vanda didn't even look down at me before she walked on. Caoin knelt at the edge, her eyes deep wells.

"Can't you keep a secret?" she asked softly, voice breaking apart.

175

Lying to her probably wouldn't have saved me from falling by that point, but I couldn't do it anyway.

"I will. I'll never say your name. But I'm sorry, I have to say something."

"No. I'm sorry," she near enough mouthed, a perfect pair of beaded tears rolling as she readied herself to leave.

"I'll do anything else you ask of me," I pleaded, my will slipping. "Anything."

She nodded resolutely then stood and turned. I watched her disappear from view. She didn't look back. I prepared myself for one last roll of the dice, a lunge for the hilt of the knife. Then, out of sight, she said one more thing, almost smothered by the wind but heard and felt deep inside, like when we were together. A whisper that hit me with more devastating force than any shout. A single word — *fall.*

XIX

So pale and cold. The silver disc could have easily been mistaken for the moon, but soon as my eyes opened I knew the sun was shining on me.

Confession. I didn't enact her last wish to the letter. I jumped.

Accepting there was no way up, I decided to go down on my own terms. Rather than wait until I couldn't hold on any longer I leapt outwards, giving myself a chance of clearing the rock and straightening up before hitting the water. Could have been near a hundred feet but it passed in a flash.

Did myself no favour by forgetting to spread my limbs once I was in, sinking faster and further than necessary, but better that over it not being deep enough. Once I'd fought my way to the surface then it really became me against the sea.

Bobbing like a rag doll, I scrabbled up a mental picture of the coastline, an overhead map not to scale. Seemed less daunting to think of the task in two legs; following the obtuse curve of the cliffs would put me in sight of the harbour. Had swum that sort of distance before but never at night, never alone.

Wanted to maintain a line not too close and not too far — avoid getting pulled out or smashed in — but it was only in my hands to a degree, the motion of the waves making a lurching zig-zag of my progress. Likewise, any idea of maintaining a formal stroke quickly fell apart, resorting to crawling on my sides, dismissing a compulsion to swim backwards for fear of losing sight of the target.

Clear perception of time was a luxury I didn't have, but estimate it took upwards of fifteen minutes to round the bend and see the glow of civilisation. Looked about twice the same length again. Powered by a gripping dread that if I stopped I wouldn't be able to start, my rhythm never broke. Almost mechanical, the physical repetition and a singular thought of just keep going combined into a trancelike state of being.

Then something strange. Whether actually in the water with me, just in my mind or even somewhere beyond, I felt a looming presence, patiently watching, waiting for me to slip into the dark. Body was ready to give in but not my spirit.

Last thing I remembered was reaching the inlet and searching for a way out of the water. Finding myself surrounded by the high walls of a canal, I'd turned in exhaustion onto my back and stretched out. Just needed a moment to gather some strength. A moment with my eyes closed.

I'd stared straight at the heavily diffused sun a good while before even trying to understand where I was. When I eventually took in the view, it was from the sodden basin of a sleeping residential street in what could only be a lower part of the Drink. I was literally lying in a ditch but it could have been worse; a couple feet to the side and I would have been in a pool of grey water the size of a shallow bath. In fact I was almost dry. Not for long though.

The wistful birdsong that led the stir of dawn was chased off by a menacing snarl. Louder it grew, harder to tell which direction it was coming from until it was right on top of me — the Lone Wolf yanking her motorbike to a stop in the puddle and showering me with a mini wave. Shadow cast long, the jaded reflection in the visor looked like a different man. Engine thrumming like it couldn't wait to get going, she gave me a small tilt of the helmet, the subtlest of nods. Letting off a parting shot, she tore away before I'd returned the gesture.

Could still faintly hear the growl after I'd hauled myself to my feet. Presumably my wallet and keys were claimed by the sea rather than some opportunist happening upon my helpless form. Only thing I had left in my pockets were the unrecognisable remains of what had been a j-card from a cassette with a little map daubed on the back, the frayed fragments taken from my palm by the mild breeze.

The dim street lights turned off in succession, drawing my attention to something of interest about them — a jerry-rigged cable running across their tops. A large crow pecking on the lamp overhead made eye contact, peering back at me before taking flight, leaving behind a mass of mangled gaffer tape and a visibly severed connection within. I grinned, thinking if only there was some way I could give Tommi a tip off. An unusual rattling sound prompted me to look down just as a can of spray paint rolled against my foot. Shaking it up, I stepped to the closest wall and drew a big 'T' and an arrow pointing skyward, with just enough red left over to sign it off with a winking smiley.

Aside from my spell in the water I was further from home than I'd been all night, but was intrigued to discover that getting there was no longer my overriding instinct. Wanted nothing more than a cup of tea and something to eat. Bim's wayward slip would have come in real handy; was probably drifting around out there somewhere. Maybe I could find a way to draw some cash though. Fuck it — rent a motel room, grab a shower and some sleep. With the exception of my brief bouts of unconsciousness I'd been awake over twenty-four hours.

Could say I was just delaying the difficult conversation I'd promised myself to have, but other than that I couldn't think of a single thing I had to get back to. With my business in town far from finished what was the rush? More's the point, got the feeling I already was home.